DANCING
WITH AN
ΔLIΞN

DANCING
WITH AN
ALIEN

by Mary Logue

HarperCollins*Publishers*

Library of Congress Cataloging-in-Publication Data
Logue, Mary
    Dancing with an alien / Mary Logue
        p.   cm.
    Summary: A teenage boy from outer space travels to earth on a mission to help save
his planet, and ultimately he falls in love, causing his mission to fail.
    ISBN 0-06-028318-1. — ISBN 0-06-028319-X (lib. bdg.)
    [1. Extraterrestrial beings—Fiction.   2. Family life—Fiction.   3. Love—Fiction]
I. Title.
PZ7.L8288   Dan 2000   99-42906
[Fic]—dc21   CIP
                                                                                  AC

Typography by Christopher Stengel
1 2 3 4 5 6 7 8 9 10
❖
First Edition

Visit us on the World Wide Web!

www.harperchildrens.com

For Pedo

DANCING
WITH AN
ΔLIEN

BRANKO

I am here.

On this very green Earth. The sun shines for fourteen hours and thirty-three minutes today. The sky is blue like they said it would be.

I am here on a mission.

The atmosphere is rich with smells, thick with water in my nose and chest, and from time to time, small, whining bugs that fly and bite. Martha, my hostess, told me they are called mosquitoes.

Martha and Fred, my host family, seem very nice but strange. Maybe all humans will be strange to me, but they flutter about me like birds. I know about birds. They were in the movies I saw. Martha is always asking me things. It tires me to talk so much. I feel exhausted from moving my mouth the way I have to in order to form these Earth words.

Martha told me that I looked like a regular teenager. Tall, skinny body, unruly hair. I have a mirror above my dresser in my new room and I stand up and look into it. My skin is possibly smoother than it should be. We worked hard on that, but it is still not quite the right surface. The only solution we came up with for my frizzy hair was to keep it cut fairly short. It's dyed the color brown.

I asked her if I was handsome. She looked me up and down. "Rugged, I'd say. And tall."

I thought mountains were rugged. But that's why I was sent—because I'm rugged. And because I'm short for my people. Not tall as Martha thinks. I am only six feet four inches tall.

Martha said she'd show me around town tomorrow. The small town of North St. Paul. We picked it because it's right on the edge of two cities—Minneapolis and St. Paul—and because the people here must be tough. They manage to live through temperatures that range from forty degrees below zero to over a hundred degrees above zero. It was near ninety degrees today, very comfortable.

Fred asked me if I wanted to go fishing.

"There's a lake a couple blocks away," he told me when I didn't say anything.

"I don't believe in fishing," I said.

"Oh." His mouth stayed in a round O shape for a while.

"We don't kill anything. Life is too precious."

"Yes, I see."

"I'd like to walk to the lake."

"Let's go now, before supper."

"I'd like that."

"Do you mind if I fish?" he asked.

"I'm not here to interfere."

They are trying hard, but they are a little afraid of me.

When we walked to the lake, I couldn't believe my eyes. The largest body of water I had ever seen. Nowhere is water allowed to pool on the surface like this back home. Fred dropped his hook into the water and I sat at the edge of the dock and stared.

The water was so beautiful. All different colors. Blue from the sky, gray from the stones, even flecks of green danced across it. Light edged its waves. The wind ruffled its surface. Ever-changing. Our life source. I gently dipped my hand into the cool liquid. What a luxury. Then I saw people were submerging their bodies in it. And no one was stopping them. They were running and thrashing around in the lake, hitting it with their arms and legs. I remembered it was called swimming.

I asked Fred if I could go in the water. He said sure.

I walked off the dock and stood at the edge of the lake. I had never had water all over my body before. When we are dirty, we use a special instrument to vacuum our bodies. Water is too precious to waste on washing. So, with great hesitation, I took my first step into the lake. It was cool and moist against my ankles. I kept walking, slow, easy steps. It was difficult to move through it. It grabbed my body, made my clothes heavy. I walked until only my head was above water. It was delicious. My body had never felt so light and cool.

My head was near the dock where Fred was fishing. He stared down at me. "Maybe you should have taken your clothes off," he said.

"All of them?" I asked.

"No, just your shoes and shirt. Do you know how to swim?"

"No, but I have read about it."

"You need to learn to swim."

I opened my mouth and took a big drink of water. Fred watched me and shook his head.

When we got home, Martha made me take off my wet clothes even though I told her they felt good.

We ate supper. I told them I did not want to eat the meat of the cow. But I liked the potatoes. They remind me of a tuber we also grow. I drank a glass of milk and ate a peanut butter cookie. The food has many flavors. Some I like and some taste like chemicals. But I will try anything except flesh.

Now the sky has turned dark and the stars are blinking in it. It looks like the same sky I have seen all my life, except the stars are moved around. Martha and Fred are sleeping. I looked into their room and they are in the same bed. I have never seen two people sleeping together. Their breathing is slow and heavy. I have heard that humans sleep up to ten hours a night. I need only four hours of resting.

In bed my body feels overloaded with the moisture in the air. I miss my home. I'm afraid of what I must try to do. Maybe they sent me here because they knew I would fail. But others have succeeded. I rub my face with my hands to calm myself.

I will take a few days to acclimatize. Then I need to begin my search. I have only a short time to do what I was sent here to do.

I am here to find a female.

☾ TONIA

Today Mom took me to buy a new bathing suit. I don't know why I let her come with me. I hate my body. It's big and hulking. Especially next to my mother's. She stands about five feet five inches tall. Perfect figure. She seems continually surprised to discover that her daughter is a hulking six feet tall and solid. She brought me these little frilly two-piece bikinis to try on. I finally went and found a gold one-piece Speedo. It fit me to a tee. I came out of the dressing room and modeled it.

"You look like you're going out for the Olympics, so athletic." My mom did not even try to keep the surprise out of her voice. My mother tends to see what she wants to see and when reality appears suddenly in front of her it is always a shock.

"Good. I want to look like that."

My little four-year-old brother, Buzz, had come with us. He looked up at me and said, "I think Tonia looks like a statue."

"You're never going to get a guy if you don't try a little," my mom said.

"What makes you think I want a guy?"

This is an ongoing discussion with my mother. She seems to feel my life won't be complete until I'm hooked at the hip to a boy. My mom and dad were married at the end of high school. I've never even had a date. They met when they were seventeen, the age I am now. My mom tells me I'm a late bloomer. When she says that it makes me think of a field full of daisies that bloom all summer long and then just when winter is about to come this poor little clump of goldenrod turns yellow for a second until the frost kills it. Needless to say, I'm the goldenrod.

"Tonia, someone is going to think you are the most wonderful girl in the world. I know it will happen."

"Mom, please . . ."

She left the dressing room and I sat on the bench and looked at myself in the mirror. My hair is getting longer. It's one of my best assets, as my mother would say, thick, straight brown with glints of red. I don't have big breasts but they're there.

And I have had boys ask me out. Tom Towwit asked me to go to the movies with him. But since he only came up to my armpit and hadn't learned how to talk to me and look at me at the same time, I turned him down. Nicely. I actually think Tom might turn into a fine man someday, but I don't need to be stuck with him in the meantime.

Why does everyone act as if you're not complete if you don't have a man by your side?

I knew I was going to have a great summer. Beatrice was coming back from camp in another few days and we would have a blast, playing chess, reading books, watching old movies.

I held up the bathing suit. I thought I looked good in

it. I decided I would get it. I liked looking like a statue or an Olympic swimmer and I liked one-pieces because they were actually made for swimming. Swimming is what I like to do when I go to the beach, unlike all the other girls who oil their bodies and paint their nails, just waiting for the boys to swarm all over them.

I would rather wait for the right one to come along.

☾ BRANKO

My feet hang off the end of the bed when I stretch out on it. It's morning and I am listening to Fred and Martha move around the house. I try to stay out of their way. I either stay in my room, studying, or I go for long walks. Yesterday, I walked to downtown St. Paul and back. Martha couldn't believe it. I find that she is often skeptical of what I say.

"There are some tall buildings down there," I said.

"Yes, but why did you go downtown? We could have driven you. That's a long way to walk."

"I like to walk. And sometimes I ran."

I have to watch how fast I run here. I know that the fastest humans can only run a mile in four minutes. I can run it in under three. So I lope. I watch my pace and I don't stride out the way I can. Actually, I'm not in very good shape. My long journey took some of the muscle out of me. It will be a while before I'm at my peak again.

I have seen some girls on my walks and runs around the town. It amazes me that they are allowed to walk around in public. Yet I knew it would be this way.

The girls often glance at me and then look away. Some of them have very big mammary glands and some of them look like boys. I try not to stare, but I cannot help myself. I have to find one who can breed. I have yet to talk to a girl.

Fred and I went to the beach again. He bought me a pair of swimming trunks yesterday. The trunks have penguins on them. This doesn't make sense to me as a penguin is an animal of the Antarctic circle. But penguins are amazingly good swimmers. Maybe I too will become a good swimmer.

Martha packed us a lunch, a "picnic" she called it, and we went to the beach. Fred has thin legs and fat feet. But he swims very well. I don't. I think my body density is too much for the water. I sink. I tried to move my arms and legs the way Fred showed me, but often I seemed to go backward instead of moving forward through the water, and always I sink.

There were many fine females at the beach today, but they are very noisy. They often shriek and run and seem to congregate in little groups, sitting on towels on the beach. They all are very beautiful to me.

What I do not understand is this—the females do not swim. They spread out big towels on the sand. Then they anoint themselves with oil and stretch out so that the sun can roast their whole bodies. From time to time, they turn over. They must turn over so they maintain a constant color. And in front of them, all this time, is the water. What keeps them from entering it? Are they afraid? I do not know whom I can ask these questions. Fred gives me a strange look when I ask him.

There is one who is different. She came down to the beach with a little boy. After spreading out her towel, she walked right into the water. I watched her swim and was very envious. She was tall with long arms and long legs and she moved through the water like an animal. She swam out to the raft and back several times.

I can't go out to the raft as the water is far over my head. I caught her looking at me as I walked through the water. She came up for air and our eyes met and then her face went back into the water. She has dark brown hair that slicked back against her cheeks as she swam. After she swam, she constructed some sort of building in the sand with the little boy.

Fred fished and I went walking through the water. I headed out toward the raft. The water was cold as it approached my navel. Then it came up to my chest. Finally the water was under my chin. I decided, no reason to stop there, and continued to walk out. The water came to my nose and then I was under. My eyes blinked. The water filled them. It wasn't dark. It was blurry. I could feel my whole head was under. I could see a herd of fish swimming toward the raft. I liked it underwater. When I had to breathe I turned around and headed back to shore. The water dropped down as I walked out of it.

I walked over to where Fred was fishing and wrapped myself in a towel. I had talked to no one at the beach. But soon I will begin to try to interact with the females.

☾ TONIA

Buzz and I went down to the beach today. I put on my new suit and brought a snack for us. Buzz loves going to the beach. The water felt great and I swam laps out to the raft and close in to shore while the lifeguard kept an eye on Buzz.

When I first arrived at the beach, several of the girls from my class waved at me. I waved back. But there was no one there who I would want to talk to. I can hardly wait till Beatrice is back from summer camp. The boys were all out at the raft, pushing each other off, even though the lifeguard yelled at them from time to time.

There was one guy who wasn't on the raft. A boy I'd never seen before. Quite tall. Gold complexion. Foreign-looking. Maybe he's a foreign exchange student. But they don't usually show up until it's almost time for school. This guy is definitely odd. He watched me swim. His eyes looked dark and hungry. It seemed to me that he was looking hard for something he needed desperately.

Buzz and I built a sand castle and this guy walked around in the deep water. I watched him out of the corner of my eye. He started to walk deeper and finally he was up to his neck in water. Buzz asked me a question and I turned to help him do something. When I looked back at the spot in the water where the strange guy had been he was gone. Only a ripple remained. I held my breath. What was he doing? How had he disappeared? Had I imagined him? Did he have supernatural powers?

Just as I was about to stand up and look for him, the top of his head appeared. Then he calmly walked out of the lake, water streaming down his body. I packed sand into the shape of a moat. I wondered what he was doing.

Maybe he doesn't know how to swim. He was with an older man. I think it was Mr. Towers, the one whose daughter disappeared a few years ago.

When Buzz and I got back from the beach, Mom was already home. She still had her work clothes on and looked wonderful. She works at an art gallery and wears suits and high heels. She was smoking, which I hadn't seen her do in a while. Two months ago she supposedly quit.

"What's up?" I asked.

"Buzzy, go up to your room and change your clothes."

When he had left the room, she pointed her cigarette at me and said, "Your father called to say he's going to be gone on a business trip for a few days."

"Oh."

"A business trip," she repeated.

I knew what she was thinking. It was the same thing I was thinking. Dad didn't usually have to go on business trips and certainly not on the spur of the moment. This had happened often in the past few months. Mom has a suspicious nature and when she suspects something, she acts on it.

"He said that he'd be home to pick up a suitcase and some clothes. I think maybe you and Buzz should go to the park."

"Mom."

"I have a few things to say to your father and I don't think you two need to hear them."

I didn't argue with her. Buzz and I left for the park. I kept him there for an hour playing on the swings. He wanted me to push him as high as the sky and I tried to do that without sending him over the top. When we walked home, I saw that Dad's car was still in the driveway.

Buzz said, "Hey, Dad's home. Let's go."

Before I could grab him he was off and running toward our house. He stopped as he got to the door. I ran up behind him and we stood there and heard some yelling. Mom was screaming, asking why he had to go and leave her, shouting that it was all just too much. Dad didn't say anything. I covered Buzz's ears and turned him back toward the street. We sat on the curb until Dad walked out of the house and into his car and drove away.

When we walked into the house, we found Mom collapsed on the floor, crying. But that's the way Mom is, very theatrical about everything. Buzz went and got her a box of Kleenex and I opened the refrigerator to see what we could have for dinner.

I couldn't stand how melodramatic Mom was. She wouldn't sit down with my dad and ask him what was going on, and he wasn't astute enough to know that he should ask her. So she yelled and he ducked out. It wasn't my fault they couldn't talk to each other. They had been doing this for a long time.

Mom walked into the kitchen and said, "He's left. I don't know if your father is coming back."

I didn't want to get into it with her, so I tried to change the subject. "Why don't you ever call him by his name, Mom?"

Mom laughed and said, "Because I guess I often think of him as your father. What's for supper?"

"How do BLTs sound?"

"Great." She watched me move around the kitchen as I got the bacon and lettuce and tomato out of the refrigerator. "Men are from a different planet, Tonia. That's all there is to it."

I nodded—but thought, even if they were there should still be a way to communicate.

BRANKO

I have explored. I have walked all over this town. I have figured out where the young females congregate. They travel in pairs or groups at the shopping malls. They hang out at the Dairy Queen, or the A&W, or at the beach. I decided to go out to the shopping mall today. Martha drove me. She insisted, even though I told her I could walk.

She stayed seated in the car, the engine running. When she turned to ask me a question, her face was stiff as if she was trying not to show any emotion. "I know I'm not supposed to ask you, I know they said you'd give us information at the end of your stay, but I just want to know . . . I miss her so much . . . have you ever seen our daughter?"

I knew this might happen. They had coached me on what to say. I was supposed to say that I had never met her, that I had heard she was happy. But I've never been good at lying. And I've never felt that any good came of it. My mission here was important and it was to save our people. I needed the goodwill of Martha and Fred. After all, the only hold we had over them was their daughter. As long as they knew they would find out more about her, they wouldn't turn on me.

"I have met her."

"Is she okay?"

"She's very healthy," I told her, which was true.

Martha touched her face as if she could see her daughter. She smiled, but her lips quivered. "Is she happy?"

"I don't feel comfortable talking about this right now. I will tell you more when I'm allowed."

Martha nodded her head rapidly.

"Your daughter is doing us a great service."

Martha nodded again, and put her hand over her mouth. "I just wish I could see her again. Once in my life."

I had to stop this. "I need to go to the mall now."

"Yes," she said, breathing in deeply. "Yes, thank you. Thank you so much. Just to know you've seen her. It means so much."

When we got to the mall, Martha had some shopping to do. She gave me a hundred dollars and suggested that I buy myself a pair of jeans. She knew I wanted to roam around the mall for a while. I was glad she wouldn't be with me.

I went and sat by a fountain in the middle of the mall. The sound of the water soothed me. I was nervous. Other men of my people had come and done what I was about to try to do. They had taught me what they knew. But they also said that Earth females were allowed a lot of freedom and could choose whom they wanted to spend time with. Their suggestions boiled down to: be funny, be appreciative, but never force anything. Back off if your suggestions are rebuffed in any way.

I had to start somewhere. So I decided to go and buy a pair of jeans. I knew that the guys were wearing them so large that they looked like someone else could fit inside also. I would try to find a pair that would be big on me. The ones Martha had bought for me were actually rather tight.

I walked into a store that sold only jeans and T-shirts called The Jean Dream. I started looking through a pile of jeans when I heard a voice behind me.

"I'd say you are a thirty-four thirty-eight."

I turned around and found a young female staring at my waist.

"You are tall," she told me.

"Yes, I know." Words came out of my mouth in slow motion.

She laughed.

I felt good about that laugh. "You are not so tall," I said as I looked down on her, guessing her height to be about five feet two inches. Too short for us.

She laughed again. "Can I help you?" she asked.

"What would you like to do?" I asked her.

"You know, help you find something?"

"I haven't lost anything."

"Duh," she said, and pointed her finger at her head.

I just stood and looked at her. I wasn't sure what she was doing.

"Are you a thirty-four thirty-eight?"

"I don't know what you mean," I admitted.

She tipped her head to one side and stared at my face. "Where are you from?"

"Romania."

"Where's that?"

"By Moldova and Bulgaria."

"You don't say."

I thought I had. "I do say."

"Thirty-four thirty-eight are the measurements for your inseam and your waist. It tells me what size jeans you would wear."

"Oh."

"Try these on." She handed me a pair of jeans.

"I would like them to be large."

"They're baggy. That's all we carry. They're cool."

"Cool. That would be nice since it is so hot." I started to take off my pants to try on the jeans.

"Stop," she said, and pointed me to a small room. "That's the dressing room."

I went into the small room and tried on the jeans. They were the right length and fit very loosely around my waist. They cost fifty-nine dollars. I bought them. The girl seemed very happy that I was buying them.

"Do you want to go get a Coke?" I asked her.

"I can't right now. I'm the only one here. I have to watch the store."

"Would you like to some other time?"

She cocked her head and looked at me. "Maybe."

"Is that maybe right in between yes and no or is it closer to one or the other?"

She laughed again. "I kinda have a boyfriend."

"You have a boyfriend?"

"In a way."

"What way?"

"We do things together."

"Like what?"

"Go blading. Mess around."

I was not sure what either of those two things were. "Could I take you out to dinner?"

"Don't you even want to know my name first?"

"Oh, of course. What is your name?"

"Betsy."

"Betsy. That's a good name."

"What's your name?"

"Branko."

"Bronco?"

"Close." I could tell it was time for me to go. She was starting to move around, folding clothes. "Can I find you here again?"

"Sure. I work here five days a week."

"Okay. Bye-bye, Betsy."

I walked back to the fountain. Pretty good, I thought. My first encounter with a female and I almost had a date. Dates are very important, my instructors told me. They are the beginning of a romance.

On the way home I asked Martha what "blading" was. She told me that it involved strapping a pair of shoes with wheels to your feet and then moving around on them. I have seen people doing that. It looks very enjoyable.

For some reason, I didn't ask her what "messing around" was. I thought I knew.

Beatrice is home. She called me this morning and I went over to her house. Mom is staying home from work today and she said I could leave Buzz with her. She's been putting on her brave face. Dad hasn't called, which isn't unusual for Dad. He is very absentminded and I can see him at the conference, totally lost in his work. But of course, Mom doesn't understand.

Beatrice looked great. Relaxed and happy. She's been gone for two weeks. She went to some camp for brainy kids. If I know her she played chess the whole time she was gone. Maybe she went on one nature hike. Now that she's back, summer is going to be a blast.

Beatrice and I have been best friends since seventh grade. We met in the hot lunch line after our math class. We both hated our math teacher. That might be too strong. As Beatrice would say, we both "detested" Mr. Steinen. Our complaint? He made us write down on paper all the steps it took us to solve a problem. I was used to doing most of it in my head. I hated writing it all down. It was boring and took far too long. Beatrice had a similar complaint. He threatened to put both of us into the remedial math class if we didn't do our work his way.

We have been best friends ever since. I like Beatrice because she doesn't like a lot of people. She's very opinionated. She doesn't care what other people think of her.

She does like me and she's a true-blue friend. Also, she's one of the smartest people I know. That includes most of our teachers.

We also share the fact that we've never been out on a date. Barely been kissed. Just at some silly parties where the boys will make out with anyone because it's in the dark. She's pretty philosophical about it. She says that they don't know what they're missing and that she's probably more suited to someone quite a bit older than her and, as long as she's wishing, rich.

When we get together we like to read books. We'll make hot chocolate and cinnamon toast and sit at opposite ends of the couch in her living room and read. Before she went off to camp she had been reading a lot of science fiction. I'm into a mystery kick myself: Agatha Christie, Dorothy Sayers, and Dashiell Hammett.

But we also stay up all night at sleepovers and talk. We talk about if there is a god and if we'll ever marry and who is the stupidest kid in school and what are the ingredients to a perfect malt.

Beatrice looks like a cute choir boy. She hates the word "cute" so she'd die if she heard me say that. She's not very tall, rather chubby, and has straight sandy-blond hair cut in a bob. She also wears glasses, wouldn't even consider contacts. She thinks glasses give her a little extra distance from the outside world. She says they even make her see better than normal people.

"What's shaking?" she asked me as I came in her back door.

"Good swimming weather," I told her.

"Oh, no. I suppose you're going to want me to accompany you to the beach again this year."

Swimming was a major point we differed on. I loved it, she detested it. But I could often persuade her to go to the beach with me if I promised we would lie in the shade on the grass, and bring lots of books to read and snacks.

"I don't know what your problem is with swimming. Just bring a book to the beach and pretend you are stretched out on the couch. What's the diff?" I asked her.

"I don't like lying around in what is about as much clothing as my underwear for everyone to see."

"We don't have to go today."

"Good. Do you want some lunch?"

"Sure."

Beatrice's parents both work, so she had the house to herself. She is an only child. I figure I almost am since Buzz is thirteen years younger than me. Technically, I could be his mother. Yugh, what a thought.

We often treat the kitchen like a science lab and do amazing experiments with food, a few of which even turn out to be edible. We love making this pudding cake where you pour batter into a pan and then the top part turns into cake and the bottom is a gooey pudding.

"What do you want to create?" I asked.

"Let's play it safe today. Grilled cheese."

Now even grilled cheese offers immense variety. Beatrice likes peanut butter in her grilled cheese, I prefer mustard. She says I have the more mature taste, which is a high compliment coming from Beatrice. We each worked on our sandwiches in separate frying pans.

"So how was camp?" I asked her, as I turned over my sandwich. Perfecto, toasted just the way I like it.

"Fab," she said, as she flipped her sandwich too.

"Great."

"Really quite fabulous."

It is unlike Beatrice to repeat herself. This unusual behavior prompted a question. "What made it so fabulous?"

"I'll tell you in a sec." She plopped her sandwich on a plate and handed me one for mine. We walked into the living room.

She picked up her sandwich, then announced casually, "Well, I met someone . . ."

I dropped my sandwich. Beatrice had thought for a moment of becoming a nun. She started reading about Hildegard von Bingen, a twelfth-century German abbess, and decided that she liked the idea of living separate from men.

"You mean of the male species?"

"This one's different."

"Oh, no. This is bad."

"Tonia, wait and listen."

"An exception?"

"I think."

"Tell."

"Well, he reads Agatha Christie."

I nodded. Good start. "Uh-huh." I decided I might as well eat my sandwich and hear her out. I took a bite. Not too bad. Maybe a tad too much mustard.

"He's not afraid to wear purple."

Beatrice's favorite color, even though it doesn't look good on her.

"He's only five feet five inches tall, so he doesn't tower over me."

"Hey, I tower over you."

"Yes, but you do it gracefully."

"Thanks."

"I've beat him at chess."

"So you're smarter than him."

"No, he's beat me at chess too. And he can read Aztec hieroglyphs and he believes there is life on other planets." She made the last statement triumphantly and proceeded to take a bite of her sandwich.

"Wow." You see, Beatrice has believed in extraterrestrials forever. Since she was born, she claims. She actually thinks she might have lived before on another planet. I don't agree with her. I neither believe nor disbelieve. I'm an agnostic about ETs. I would have to see one to believe in them. But I knew how important this issue was for Beatrice. I got ready for the big question. "So did you guys lipsuck?"

"You make it sound so gross."

"Hey." I jumped up off the couch. I felt really deserted by my best friend. "You were the one who coined that word. And now you've gone and done it."

"I didn't say I did."

"No, but you didn't say you didn't."

She took another bite of her sandwich and then said slowly, "I think you might like it."

"Oh, so now you're the expert."

"Well, you're the body person. You love to swim. You're into pleasure. And I do think this is big-time pleasure."

With this last revelation, we both finished up our sandwiches, not saying anything. I was worried that Beatrice would spend all her time this summer with this guy and I'd have no one.

But she is my friend, so I asked, "What's his name?"

"Walter."

"Good name."

"Suits him." I could tell she was trying to hold herself in, but she did so want to talk about him. "He lives in White Bear Lake."

Only the next school district over, so he was very close.

"But he stayed on at camp for another week."

That was good news. "Oh. That's too bad."

"It will be hard," she admitted. "But we decided the separation might be good for us."

I walked home from her house feeling dejected. There was a very small part of me that was glad for Beatrice. I knew that she didn't really want to be celibate the rest of her life. But I thought she'd wait for me to find someone too. I don't know. I thought we'd do this together like we did everything together. It would be awful if I had to spend the rest of the summer alone.

☽ BRANKO

I've been reading a lot about sex. I found some books in Martha and Fred's library that seem to be stories of different people's lives. These stories go into all aspects of someone's existence and this often includes sex. It's called fiction. Made-up stories. Funny to read books that are just about people. I have never done that before. All the books I read are usually about research, to learn. But I view these books as research.

What I have learned is that here on Earth, when people grow up and get married or even don't get married or are married to different people, they have sex very often. Whenever they feel like it. There is no ritual, no research, no tests or studies being done. They just lie together in bed and have sex. Sometimes they are not even in a bed.

It has made me feel rather funny about Fred and Martha. I mean, they are lying together in bed every night. So they are probably having sex all the time. Whenever I look in on them, they are sleeping.

Then, the other night, I stayed up late and watched a video Fred had rented. And I saw people having sex. They rub their skin together, they move their mouths over each other's mouths. They groan and make faces. Sometimes they look like they are going to die.

I wondered if I would get to have sex. It made me feel so odd to think about it. My skin got all hot and I didn't know what to do with my hands. My instructors talked about sex a little. They said it was okay to do it, but not to push it on the female. Let her do the advancing.

Only a select few males get to have sex back home. And when they do, they must be watched and studied. The results must be shown to be positive. It is considered a great honor to be allowed to procreate.

I can't believe what happened today. I'm still totally hyper about it. My body is zinging with adrenaline.

I actually persuaded Beatrice to go to the beach with me. I think she knows I feel a little bad about her and Walter and so she's trying to be really nice to me. I'll take it. We packed a big lunch, brought books and magazines, even a chessboard, and found a perfect spot in the shade.

It was a great day. Eighty-five degrees. Not a cloud in the sky. A soft breeze through the trees. Very comfortable. Beatrice even went wading. She was wearing a new bathing suit.

"Walter says he likes my body just the way it is," Beatrice announced, as we were walking through the water, trying to pick up rocks with our toes.

"Your body is fine."

"You don't think I'm too fat."

I turned in horror at her. "Beatrice, you've never said that word before. You hate girls who try to diet. What's going on with you?"

Her eyes squinted and she shook her head as if trying to rid herself of a fly. "I don't know. I've never felt like this before. I don't know that I like it. All of a sudden I care about what I look like."

"Hey, that's fine. Just don't go overboard. I mean, I think you can be a staunch feminist and still want to look nice. But being the size of a toothpick isn't attractive."

"I know. I kind of miss Walter. We saw each other every day. And now I haven't talked to him in a couple days. It's not easy to get to use a phone at camp. It just about has to be an emergency. But I'm worried. What if he doesn't like me anymore when he comes home?"

"I thought you guys were friends."

"We are."

"Well, so friends always like friends. That doesn't go away. Don't go and flip out on me. I'm having enough trouble seeing you with a guy without having to deal with you being moony about him."

"You're right. You want to play chess?"

"So you can beat me?"

Beatrice looked up and smiled. "Well, that will make me feel better."

We played a good game and then ate our sandwiches and Twinkies. Beatrice was reading in the shade when I went down to swim out to the raft a few times. The water felt great, like smooth silk on my skin. Beatrice was right. I do love to feel my body. Maybe I would like kissing and all that. Who knows?

So I swam out to the raft and pulled myself up onto it to take a break. As I watched the shore I noticed that tall dark boy who I had seen here before. He was doing the same thing he did last time. So strange. He would walk out into deep water and then walk back in. Walk back out and walk around with his nostrils just above the water line like a periscope, his eyes scanning the surface of the water. I wondered what the story was with him.

Then, all of a sudden, he did something different. He jumped up and aimed toward the raft. He started thrashing his arms and legs in the water. It looked like he was trying to swim. And he actually was getting someplace. He probably moved a yard or two toward the raft. Then he sank. The water surface cleared. There was no sign of him. I waited. Air bubbles. He didn't come up. I saw a finger break the surface, but then it sank. I waited one more second and then I jumped in.

I had taken senior lifesaving and I knew the motto: "Reach, throw, row, go." There was nothing to reach this guy with, nothing to throw from the raft, no boat available to row out to him. So I was going. I hoped I could find him.

I did the lifesaver's jump into the water. It's like a modified belly flop so your head doesn't go below water and you can keep your eyes on the spot the person went down. I swam to the spot and dove.

At first I couldn't find him. I came up for air, took a deep breath, and went down again. I dove to the bottom of the lake and just as my lungs were bursting I found him. He was heavy. I wrapped my arms under his arms from behind and pushed off the bottom. We were not in deep water and that helped.

When I got him up to the surface of the water, I wrapped an arm around him, over his chest, and started to swim in with him. I only had to go a few yards and I could touch. He wasn't breathing that I could tell. My heart flopped around inside my chest like a fish. People were running out from the shore. The lifeguard, a girl named Sara, came out to help me. She was a big blonde and between the two of us we dragged him to shore. Although I probably should have let her take over, I knew what to do and I did it. I turned the guy on his stomach and pounded him on the back. Sara helped me.

Then I laid him faceup. I pinched his nose and cupped his chin in my hand. I wanted him to live so bad I was shaking. Please, I thought, please come back. Breathe. I put my lips to his and breathed into him. My air moved into his mouth and when I had no more, I turned my head to the side and listened. I did it again. I breathed like this for a while and then he started to do it with me. I couldn't stop. We were breathing together. When he was going strong, I just held him in my arms and let him breathe.

He was like a huge animal, a big warm animal that I had saved. His body was smooth and soft. He was shivering and I kept an arm around him. Then he opened his eyes. They were unlike any eyes I had ever seen before. They were brown. And maybe if you weren't close to them, they would just look brown. But I was very close and I could see that they had flecks of red in them. And instead of just the darkness of the pupil, there were rings around it before the iris started.

His eyes looked like a cat's-eye marble. They glistened and shone in the sun like a jewel. Then he smiled up at me and said a word I had never heard before. It sounded like birdsong; it started high and went low and it entered my heart. Then he shook his head and said, "Thank you."

☾ BRANKO

I have found her.

The perfect female.

She gave me life. She brought me back.

I had seen her at the beach before. Since then, Fred has been working hard on my swimming. I felt like I was getting someplace. So when I saw her swim out to the raft, I decided to try to go there too.

I walked out as far as I could touch and then I launched myself toward the raft. I swam. I know I swam at least a few paces. I could see the raft getting closer. She was watching me. Then I couldn't swim anymore. My arms were too heavy, my feet were sinking and dragging me down. I tried to reach out my hand for another stroke but I was sinking.

I went down into the water and it was very quiet. I was scared, but I also liked the feeling. The water was all around me. I had my eyes open and I could see the light filtering down from above. The water was way over my head. I couldn't even reach the surface with my hand. I tried to jump, but I didn't get very far. Then I made the mistake of trying to breath in the water. I choked. The world turned black. I curled up and faded away.

The next thing I knew I was being held and someone was blowing wonderful air into me. Someone was holding me like I was a baby and I knew I was safe. I knew I was alive again. Then I opened my eyes and she was there. So big. So warm. She had given me everything. I never wanted to leave her arms. In that moment, I made a mistake. I said a word in my language. I hope she did not notice. Then I thanked her.

A man came over to help and tried to take me to the hospital. The girl was pushed aside. Fred came running over. But I couldn't go to the hospital. They would know if they saw me that I wasn't one of them. I stood up even though the world spun around me. I told them I was fine. I leaned on Fred and told him we had to go home. I left the girl there. I don't know who she is. I don't know her name. But I will find her. She saved me. I must see her again.

☾ TONIA

When I got home from the beach, Dad was there, sitting in his usual chair in the living room.

"How's the water?" he asked.

"Great. How's the weekend?" I asked.

"Fine. I got my business taken care of."

"Where's Mom?"

"She's cooking dinner."

And she was cooking dinner, singing as she threw together fettucine alfredo, my father's favorite dish. They must have made up.

"I saved a guy's life today," I mentioned.

My father stood up and walked over to me. "Tonia, what happened?"

I shrugged my shoulders. "This guy went in a little too deep and I had to pull him out. I was closer than the lifeguard. No big deal."

He threw his arms around me. "You are something else, my Tonia. You are meant for big things." He kissed me on the head.

Buzz came running in at that moment and banged into my legs with his head. Mom walked into the doorway of the living room and waved at me. We were all glad to be a happy family again. I wondered how long it would last. I don't like it when my father is gone. It allows my mother's imagination to run wild.

That night, I couldn't get to sleep. I kept reliving rescuing the smooth-skinned man. I'd shut my eyes and he would be drowning again. A nightmare. I thought of him as a man, not a boy. I remembered holding him in my arms. I wondered who he was, what he was doing here.

He didn't seem like he was born in Minnesota. He looked different from everyone here. More dense, more animal, slightly unhuman. On the way home from the beach, Beatrice had said as much, only in her own words. "He certainly has a presence, even when he's drowning." Then she added, "He scares me a little."

"I know. Me too."

"Something is weird about him. He's bigger than real life. Like from a movie. He's an exaggeration of a normal guy."

I didn't make a crack about her size. Beatrice is sensitive about only being five feet two inches tall. But the golden man towered over me so he must seem huge to her.

I had never held a man in my arms before, except my dad and my brother. I felt like we had a connection now. I wondered what it would be like to see him again. I wondered if I would.

Just as I was drifting off to sleep, I heard him thanking me and then I heard the other word he said to me. It flitted in my ear like a sound from the air itself, a trill from somewhere I'd never been.

BRANKO

"But I have to find her," I told Fred.

"She lives around here. I've seen her before." Fred kept watching TV. He didn't want to talk to me.

"You don't know who she is?"

He turned toward me and gave me a dark look. "I don't keep up with the kids anymore. Not since my daughter is gone."

I nodded. "I understand. But how should I find her?"

"My job is to take care of you. Feed you and house you. I'm doing that. Keep me out of the rest of it." He reached over and turned the TV up louder.

After my accident this afternoon, I had rested in my room until dinner. Martha kept coming in and checking on me. I told her I was feeling healthy again. Finally, I sat up and stared out the window. Now the sun was sinking into a bed of clouds and turning them all rose-colored.

I had to do something. I couldn't sit still. I had found the female I wanted. She was nearby. I decided to go and look for her.

After dark in North St. Paul, people sit inside their houses and watch TV or do the dishes. Some of them put themselves in a comfortable chair and read. They turn on all the lights in their house and leave their windows clear. It is very easy to see them as you walk by on the empty streets. It is like they are captive animals on display.

I went first to the beach. I knew she wouldn't be there, but I wanted to remember what had happened. Since my mother died, it was the first time a woman has held me. I walked down to the sand and sniffed. Just a faint fish smell. Nothing significant.

The streets in this area are laid out in a grid. I walked up and down the north-south streets and then I turned and walked the east-west streets. Looking in windows, I saw a girl brushing her dog, a woman walking across a room with a baby on her shoulder, a man screaming at the TV. The windows let me look in.

I saw so much life going on.

I studied and searched. My quest.

Females with long blond hair, with short red hair, with braids, but no tall female with dark brown hair and large arms. No savior girl. She was not in any of the windows. So, for me, they were empty.

I walked until the lights went out. I walked until the stars were almost as bright as the streetlights. I thought of the girl who had saved me and wondered what I would do if I found her. Maybe I would ask her to save me again.

☾ TONIA

Beatrice is in a tizzy. My dear friend whom I thought I knew so well has been transformed into a normal teenage girl who has a major crush on a boy. I would have never thought it possible. But I'm seeing it with my own eyes. Beatrice actually tried to outline her own eyes with a pencil to make them look bigger.

"But they are already huge," I told her.

"Oh." She looked at herself in the mirror.

"And you smudged the pencil so much you look like a clown."

"Can't you help?" she asked and held the pencil out to me.

"I like you the way you are. You don't need to wear makeup. Did you ever wear makeup at camp?"

"Well, no."

"So stop being a weirdo. Walter likes you the way you are. So do I. Calm down."

"Okay." She put the pencil down.

"Are you sure you want me to be here?" I asked.

"Yes, absolutely." She bent over the sink and washed her face.

The plan was, Walter was coming over at noon and we were going to go get a pizza at North St. Paul Pizza, which made the best pizza in the world. He had his parents' car, so then we thought maybe we'd just drive around for a while.

When I first saw Walter I have to say that I was slightly disappointed. He was more than half a foot shorter than me, which still made him three inches taller than Beatrice, and he was as solid around as a garbage can. His hair was thin and stuck straight up and he wore glasses that slid down his nose. He walked funny as if he were always hitching up his underpants.

But when he smiled you noticed that his eyes were very bright and his teeth were straight and clean and his mouth had a nice shape to it. When you ignored the package that Walter came in, he was almost attractive.

He got out of his car and walked across the lawn, and Beatrice went out to greet him. They met in the middle of the lawn and then didn't know what to do. She reached out and petted him on the shoulder and he rubbed her on the head. Then they each took a step back as if that had been too personal. Then they both smiled at each other and that's when I saw that Walter had his own form of cuteness. That's when I started to like him.

Beatrice turned around and waved at me to come out and meet him.

I walked out of the house feeling like Dorothy in the land of the Munchkins. "Hi," I said, and looked down at him.

"The beautiful Amazon," he said, and stuck out a very solid hand for me to shake.

Then we all piled into his parents' Saab and drove down to the pizza place. Walter pushed buttons to roll down all the windows and cranked up the music in the CD player super-loud. It was great—music and air streaming all around us.

North St. Paul Pizza is an institution. It's where everyone goes to celebrate anything: birthdays, graduation, finals, you name it. The place is nothing to look at. Four booths line the far wall with old linoleum on the tables and the benches painted red. A jukebox sits near the window, and tables are scattered in the remaining room. All the energy is put into producing a wonderful product—the perfect pizza. Beatrice and I both like the vegetarian special—olives, green peppers, mushrooms—but then we have them add one more ingredient, anchovies. That little salty fish makes my taste buds water up just thinking about it.

We took a booth. Walter and Beatrice sat next to each other, kind of close. Beatrice actually picked up a menu and handed it to Walter. I thought, what do we need menus for? We know what we're getting.

She said to him, "What kind of pizza do you like?" Then she asked him, "Do you like pizza?"

I was horrified. These things should all be worked out early on in a relationship. But then I realized they probably hadn't had pizza up at camp. They probably just ate beans and wienies.

Walter stared at the menu, but I could tell he wasn't reading it. He knew he had been put to the test. So after a moment or two of fake staring, he looked up at Beatrice and said, "I love pizza. What kind do you like?"

Beatrice fluttered. Her hands actually did a little dance in the air. "There's not much I don't like."

"Except cow," I muttered. "And pig." He had to know that she absolutely refused to eat meat.

"Well." Walter gathered himself together. "I like mushroom."

Beatrice chirped. "So do I." She pointed at the menu. "They have a vegetarian special that's quite good."

Walter beamed with relief. "That sounds great."

He thought he had passed the test, but I couldn't let him get away so easy. I said, "How about anchovies?"

Their two faces lifted to me like two suns rising across the top of the booth. Beatrice's face had a hint of a frown on it and Walter's was filled with wonder. "Anchovies?" he asked.

"Yeah. We like anchovies on our pizza." I was feeling a little possessive of Beatrice, and it surprised me.

"Hey, I'll try anchovies. I've never had them." He laughed, then added, "There isn't much I don't like to eat."

I'm not sure that Walter liked anchovies, but he ate them. I guess he passed the test. The pizza was as good as always: crisp crust, generous portions of veggies, fresh mushrooms, spicy tomato sauce, and a thin coating of cheese, not too thick. You didn't feel all bloated when you were done eating it; you felt like you wanted to go out and have fun. So we did.

We got back in the car and needed a destination. I

was beginning to feel very much like the third wheel on a bicycle, but I also knew that Beatrice would feel bad if I went home too soon.

Beatrice suggested driving down to the lake. It was one of the prettiest spots in North St. Paul. At night kids went and parked there, but I assumed that wouldn't happen since it was broad daylight. We didn't have our swimsuits and I knew Beatrice didn't want to go swimming, so I didn't even suggest it.

On our way there, Beatrice pointed out the spots of interest: the big white twenty-foot-tall polar bear statue from the local winter carnival, the high school we went to, which had been an elementary school and some of the drinking fountains were at about knee-high level, the Dairy Queen, another of our favorite snacking spots. Last summer Beatrice and I had eaten our way through every single ice cream concoction on the menu, item by item.

During a lull in conversation, Beatrice mentioned my rescue.

"You saved someone from drowning?" Walter turned around to look at me and we headed toward the curb. Then he turned back and swerved safely down the street again.

"Well, kind of."

"Absolutely," Beatrice said. "That guy was a goner. No one else could have saved him. He's huge and an even worse swimmer than me."

I found I didn't want to talk about what had happened. It was too important to me. If we talked about it, it would turn into something normal. But when I thought about it in my mind, saving him was huge. Bigger than anything that had ever happened to me before.

"Wow," Walter said. "I took junior lifesaving, but I guess I never thought it would really happen."

"It was no big deal," I said. "He just got up and walked away." And, I thought, I don't even know who he is. "So, Walter, how did you and Beatrice meet?"

When I saw the back of his neck redden, I knew he was blushing. "We bumped into each other in the middle of the night."

Beatrice started laughing and explained, "Didn't I tell you? I was on my way to the craphole, that's what we call it at camp, and Walter was on his way back and we both were shining our flashlights right in front of our feet and literally ran into each other. We ended up talking for an hour right there on the path. We were immediately *simpatico*."

Right then we arrived at the beach. I was glad, because I wasn't sure how much more of the mush stuff I could take. As I looked down at the beach, I wished I had brought my swimsuit. The water looked perfect, a sheet of blue glass with nary a ripple. I love swimming in the late afternoon, when the water is the warmest it will be and the wind has died down. There were a few kids playing in the water, two girls were lying on the raft, a couple moms were stretched out on the beach reading books, and the lifeguard was sitting back in her chair wearing a big floppy hat.

Then a shadow moved under a tree.

BRANKO

I went back to the beach the next day. I couldn't help it. I hoped that if she had thought about me at all, wondered about seeing me again, remembered what had happened, she would go down to the beach. Or she would be at the beach because that's where she liked to be. I had seen her there twice. If I went often enough I'd see her again.

I didn't feel ready to go back in the water, so I sat in the shade of a tree and watched the beach. The water was so calm. It looked like I could walk on it. But I didn't believe that after almost drowning in it yesterday.

Then, just when I was thinking of going home, I saw her. She was with another girl and a boy. They were laughing and talking together. None of them was dressed for swimming. I stood up and walked over to talk to her.

As I approached them, they grew silent. My rescuer stared at me and I stared back. She was as beautiful as I had remembered. Large and strong with dark hair and eyes that held the water of the lake. I stopped in front of her and touched her on the forehead with the palm of my hand. It was what we did at home, a gesture of thanks and praise. I knew I shouldn't do it. It was not appropriate behavior for this land, but I couldn't stop myself. It was so important to me that she know how I felt about her.

"I am Branko," I said. "And I need to thank you and to know your name."

She looked back at the boy and girl and then turned back to me. "Antonia, but everyone calls me Tonia."

"Tonia." I copied her voice, tried to say it like she had. It had a nice sound.

"Where are you from?" she asked me.

I stood very still and looked into her eyes. "I'm not from here," I said.

"I can tell," she said.

Then I told her what I'd been taught to say. "I'm from Romania. I'm just visiting some people for the summer."

"Are you going to go to school?"

"No. I won't be here that long."

She gestured back at the two people behind her, "This is my best friend, Beatrice, and her new friend Walter."

"Beatrice and Walter," I repeated. "Are you on a date?"

They all laughed when I said that. I wasn't sure what was so funny but I tried to laugh too. Beatrice said, "Not really. We're just hanging out."

Again, I wasn't sure of the meaning of her words, but I nodded my head and repeated them. "Hanging out?"

"Yeah, we wanted to show Walter the lake."

I turned to look at the lake. "It is a very great lake, but can be dangerous."

"You need to learn how to swim," Tonia said to me.

"Can you teach me?"

She hesitated, but Beatrice answered, "Sure she can."

Tonia hid her head for a second, then lifted her eyes again and said, "I could try."

I started to take off my shirt.

"Not now." She laughed and put out a hand to stop me from disrobing. "We can set a date."

"We can go on a date?" I asked, happy with how fast this was moving.

Now they were all laughing again.

"I meant a time to teach you to swim. Not a date."

"But I would like a date too," I told her.

"That's not part of the deal."

"How about tomorrow for the swimming?"

She shook her head. "I have to watch my brother."

"The day after."

"That would be fine." She added, "We can meet here at three. That's when my mom gets home."

"At three o'clock in the afternoon?" I asked.

"Yes."

"Here at the beach?" I wanted to be sure I got it right. "Tonia?"

"Yes."

"And you will teach me to swim?"

She laughed. "I don't want to have to rescue you again."

"I wouldn't mind."

The girl named Beatrice stepped forward. She had blond hair that was the color of a sunflower and wore glasses over her eyes. She came up to my armpit and was a little portly. She addressed me with much conviction. "Tonia saved your life yesterday, didn't she?"

"Yes. She did."

Now the boy Walter joined in the conversation. "Did you think you were facing death?"

"I felt like it was in the water with me. Very close. But I wasn't afraid of it."

"Cool," Walter said.

"Actually," I explained, "the water was fairly warm."

"Do you believe in life after death?" Beatrice asked.

I liked them. I liked their questions. "Yes, but not in this same form."

Walter nodded his head. "Possibly you have something there."

"Good luck with your swimming lessons," Beatrice said.

They all said good-bye to me, and Walter stuck out his hand. I grabbed it as I had seen people do and we shook our hands up and down together. Tonia touched me on the shoulder and it gave me a shiver. Scary that a single touch could affect me like that. I walked home thinking about my swimming lessons. But the main thing I thought about was that I was going to see her again. And I would ask her for a date. We would talk and maybe hold hands.

I had chosen her. I knew she was the right one. She was everything we were looking for in a female. She was as good a specimen as anyone had brought back to our planet yet. With her size and her energy, she would be perfect. I would be a hero when I returned home.

"Where's Mom?" I asked, as I came in the door just before dinnertime.

My dad was stirring a pan of macaroni and my brother had turned the block of cheese into some kind of machine and was driving it around the kitchen table.

"She didn't tell me where she was going."

"Dad, have you two had a fight again?"

He stopped stirring for a moment to look at me. His eyes were sad, but he smiled. "I guess so."

"Let me do that." I took the spoon away from him. "You don't need to stir the macaroni until you put the cheese in."

"I put it in."

"You don't put it in until after you dump the water out." I was tempted to throw out the mess in the pan. I felt the cheese form at the bottom of the pan. But when I tested one of the noodles, it was nearly cooked. I poured off the water, added some milk and butter, and managed to pull the cheese back out of its globular form.

When we all sat down to eat, I quizzed my father more about my mother's whereabouts. "Did she pack a suitcase?"

"No."

"Was she mad when she left?"

"In a manner of speaking."

"Describe."

He set his fork down and spoke carefully. "Sparks were flying out of her mouth and she nearly threw a knife at me."

Buzz burst out laughing and a few noodles came flying out of his mouth. "She slammed the door," he told me when he calmed down.

"What did you do?" I asked my father.

"Nothing that I know of," he said calmly.

"Dad, think. It has to be something."

"It's a puzzle. I came in the door. I told her she looked nice, which she did. I asked how her day had gone. She told me. Then I mentioned that I had another conference I had to attend in a few weeks. Asked her what was for dinner. Then she blew up. That was it."

"It was the conference."

"I can hardly believe that. I always thought your mother liked it when I went away. She complained that I did it so seldom."

"Well, maybe you've been doing it too much lately." I didn't want to say anything more. I supposed I could have asked my father right then and there if he was having an affair, but my mother needed to be the one to do that.

We all finished our macaroni and cheese and looked at each other. It wasn't much of a meal.

Buzz stated it perfectly. "I'm still hungry."

I nodded my head in agreement.

"How does a Dilly Bar sound to you?"

We all piled into the car and headed for the Dairy Queen. My dad loves ice cream more than anyone I know. He bought a Buster Bar, I got a chocolate-dip cone with crunchies, and Buzz got a Dilly Bar, because he didn't know any better. We sat outside on one of the cement benches and ate them.

"Dad, how did you know when you met Mom that she was the one you wanted to marry?"

After taking a large bite of his bar and swallowing it, he said, "Because she told me."

"Sounds like Mom."

"I guess I just thought I'd never get that lucky again."

"How did you meet?" I asked him.

"We had our lockers right next to each other."

"So?"

"Well, one day after school she was complaining that she couldn't understand her math assignment. I was in her class. I said it was easy. She invited me over to show her how easy it was."

"So you kind of saved her?"

"In a way."

"And do you think she was indebted to you?"

"I suppose."

"Is that why she went out with you?"

Dad chewed on the stick of his Buster Bar to get the last bits of chocolate off of it. "No. She said she liked the way I looked at the world."

Buzz had dripped his ice cream down the front of his

favorite dinosaur T-shirt. I wiped it off with napkins. We all got back in the car.

On the way home I asked my father if he was glad he married my mother so young. They had been right out of high school. "We were in love. It seemed the thing to do."

The thought of my parents at my age and in love was illuminating. It went a long way toward explaining why they were still together. "What if I met someone that I fell in love with. Would you let me get married so young?"

"Why? Have you met someone you like?"

"No way." As I said the words, I thought of Branko. "Don't you know your daughter's the ugly duckling?"

My father smiled. "You have already started to transform and you don't even know it."

☾ BRANKO

My instructors always said, take it slow. They said women are like shy animals, they are the most curious about you when you walk away from them. They said, the less you tell them the better. I knew all of these lessons. I thought I was ready to pursue a female. But now I wasn't sure. I wanted to tell her everything. I was sure she would understand. But I had been taught to know better.

So I decided that during the swimming lessons, I should concentrate on learning to swim. I would never get another chance to swim again in my life. Where I came from water was rationed out. Everyone got just enough to drink a day. When it rained, the few times it did a year, people would stand outside naked and let the water run down them and pray for more. It was a holy time.

And here I was able to totally immerse myself in water and learn to move through it. I must enjoy this. I would have something to tell my people.

Tonia was at the beach before me. This was a good sign. She too was anxious. She was stretched out on a towel. Her body was bare except for the blue swimsuit she wore. When she saw me she waved but did not stand up. I came to a stop next to her and waited.

"I just had something to eat. Let's wait a few minutes before we go in the water," she said, and patted the sand next to her.

"Would you like me to sit down next to you?" I asked.

"That would be nice." When she smiled, she showed many of her teeth.

I sat down and realized she was looking at me, waiting for me to speak. I asked the question that starts most conversations in my land. "How is your father?"

She wrinkled her nose, then said, "He's okay. I don't know what he's up to."

And then I asked a question that never gets asked in my world, because there are none. "And your mother?"

"Oh, she and my dad are fighting and so she went to her mother's for a few days."

"Her mother is still alive?"

"Yeah, Granny is eighty-two and she still likes to golf."

"What an extraordinary woman. It must run in your family to have such strong women."

"I guess."

"What are your parents fighting about?"

"Well, my mom thinks my dad is seeing someone else. My dad doesn't have a clue what's going on. Which doesn't mean he isn't seeing someone else."

I didn't know what she was talking about, "seeing someone else." Didn't we all see many people during the day? Maybe it meant that he looked at her mother and thought she was someone else. I would just have to ask. "What does seeing someone else mean?"

"You know. My dad might be hanging out with

another woman. My mother is jealous. Doesn't that happen in your country?"

I thought of my land of lonesome men. "Not so much," I said.

"I think you're lucky then."

"Not very lucky," I told her.

She sat up and wrapped her arms around her knees and tossed her hair. "I'd like to hear about your country."

"It is very far away. People are poor there. I am very lucky to be able to come to visit you." I didn't want to elaborate. Again, my instructors had given me much information about the country, but advised me to speak little about it.

"You never learned to swim in Romania?"

"No, we don't do that much."

"Is it colder than here?"

"Yes, and the summers are shorter."

"Oh, that explains it. By the time the water's warm enough to swim, the summer's almost over."

"Something like that."

Suddenly she jumped to her feet. "I thought we'd work on floating and kicking today."

I jumped to my feet too. "Floating and kicking."

Now, this next part is like a dream to me. Tonia and I walked into the water together. When it was up to my waist, she told me to take a deep breath, to bend over backward and pretend I was sleeping on top of the water. Her hands came underneath me to hold me up. It was easier than I thought. The next thing I knew I was in her arms again, and in the cool embrace of the water. I could have stayed there forever. Then suddenly she took her arms away and my body buckled. I folded in the middle and water came into my nose and mouth and eyes. I came up sputtering.

"I thought you said no more drowning," I said.

"You have to keep stretched out straight. When I let go of you, don't collapse. Let's do it again and this time I will warn you when I am going to let go."

Once again I stretched out on top of the water. The sun hit my eyes and I closed them to feel the floating that I was supposed to do. Tonia told me to arch my back. She put her hands there to help me. She told me to let my feet dangle, to take deep breaths and try to keep my chest inflated, to tip my head back, to hold my arms above my head. She bent close over me and instructed me. Then, in a whisper, she said, "And now I will pull my hands away." I felt them leave me. And I continued to be held up by the water. I floated and I felt like nothing would ever hurt me. I knew she was near and watching. I was floating.

☽ TONIA

I decided to teach my brother how to swim this year. So far he's learned how to float. His thin little body weighs nothing in my arms. And now I am teaching this enormous person how to stay afloat in the water. It's amazing how strong water is. I tend to think of it as gentle and soft. But when I made Branko stretch out on the water, it held him up. He almost looked like he was going to fall asleep.

He is such a strange man. Sometimes he seems very intelligent, like he knows more than he should, and sometimes he doesn't understand the simplest thing. He can be offensive and then totally charming. He makes me laugh, yet he seems to carry around in him some huge sadness. I sense all these contradictions and never know what to expect from him. I was nervous to teach him to swim, to hold him, but when I started doing it, it felt completely natural.

When we were standing in the water, after he had learned to float, he was so happy. He was doing a dance in the water, kicking and splashing. When he calmed down, he started to thank me. "I thank you as many times as there are stars in the sky."

"You're welcome."

"You are such a beautiful woman." He looked me up and down and I felt like submerging myself in the water.

"Thank you."

"So strong and I like your breasts."

I must have given him a weird look.

"I shouldn't like your breasts?" he asked.

"Well, you can like them, but you shouldn't tell me."

"Oh, it should be a secret."

"Well, people just don't talk much about breasts."

He pointed at them. "That must be hard since they are right in front of you all the time."

"It just isn't considered polite."

"Not good manners?" he asked.

"Right."

"But if we were married, could I say I liked your breasts?"

I started to laugh. I couldn't help it. He was totally serious and trying so hard to understand that there was no way I could be mad at him. "Yes. And I would take it as a compliment."

"You should, beautiful Tonia. Now, you are going to teach me the kicking?"

Kicking was harder for him. He wouldn't always point his toes and sometimes he would actually move backward in the water. I took him to the shallow part of the beach and had him work there. He kicked and kicked, waves surging up around him. Most guys would have felt weird kicking like that at the beach, but he didn't seem to notice.

The last thing I wanted to teach him was how to

breathe in the water. So I had him blow bubbles. We went out into deeper water and sat on the pebbly bottom of the lake and took breaths and blew bubbles. Then I made him do it with his whole face in the water. He wanted to jerk his head out, so I told him to slow down and relax. We had a contest to see who could hold our breath underwater the longest. He couldn't believe it when I beat him.

"You are the best," he said.

We were sitting right next to each other and then he did a very odd thing. He held me by the shoulders and put his face very close to mine, looking me straight in the eyes, and then he rubbed his nose on my nose, both sides. I didn't know what to say. What was the weirdest of all was that I liked it.

☽ (BRANKO

It isn't the way I thought it would be. I saw this trip as a mission. I would find the female, conquer her, and bring her back home. It is not so simple, I see now. How to begin to tell her who I am, what I need from her? What if I cannot even bring myself to ask her to come with me? What if I fail at my mission?

This is such an awful thought that my very bones shake. My life will be worth very little if I do not bring back a female.

Tonia is a complicated being. I seem to change when I am around her. This I do not understand.

I have become weak. I do foolish things. I nearly drowned myself just to impress her. And I keep wanting to touch her, to make sure she's real, to have a connection with her.

I'm sitting in my room with my feet hanging over the end of my bed, staring at the ceiling. They sprayed the ceilings in this house with a white plaster that has sparkles in it, and peaks and valleys. I could stare at it forever and think of Tonia. I have this dream that she and I would go for a long walk along the ocean for miles and miles. We would walk and I would tell her everything: about the plague, about my mother's death, about the impending doom of my planet, about my mission.

But I have been warned to do none of that.

I knew when I came that this would be a dangerous mission. But I thought the danger would be from someone discovering the truth about me. Or I thought perhaps I would fail and have to go home in disgrace. I never dreamed that the worst danger to me would come from the very female I have found.

I don't even know what to say to her sometimes. I keep feeling like talking to her in my language. Then I could explain everything. I feel like I'm three years old again and I'm just learning to talk. When I was preparing to come to Earth, I watched many films and took classes on how to fit in, but nothing prepared me for Tonia.

So I decided I needed to watch more movies—to find one that would show me how to win a female. I turned on the TV and watched show after show of people trying to meet other people. When they are in love, they fight. When they're not in love, they flirt. I could never fight with Tonia.

Past midnight, Fred came in and sat down. "Can't sleep?" he asked me.

I turned the TV off. "I don't sleep very much."

"So I've noticed." He sat there with his hair sticking up from his forehead and his striped pajamas twisted around his body.

"Were you trying to sleep?" I asked. "Did I wake you up?"

He waved his hand at me. "I guess I couldn't sleep tonight either. Martha's been pestering me to ask you about our daughter."

"But you know I'm not to tell you anything until it's time for me to leave."

"Yes, but we can't help it."

I watched him. "Why not?"

"Because she is our only daughter. Our only child. Because we love her so much."

He said the words quietly. They floated out into the air between us. I could not ignore them. Suddenly, I knew what he felt. What would I do if I could never see Tonia again? It seemed an impossible thought.

I looked him in the eyes and said, "What would you like to know?"

"Anything, everything. Is she happy? Is she healthy? How is Zoran treating her?"

I would not tell him everything. He would not be able to handle it. But I would tell him what I could that would still be the truth and not hurt him. "She is very revered in our society. I don't know if she's happy. I don't really know her. I've only met her once. It would be hard for me to say."

"Yes, of course. Martha gets so upset that we can never see her. I try to imagine that she has in fact moved to Romania. That maybe sometime we will get the chance to see her or she will be able to visit. It's a possibility. After all, you came here. Maybe she could come."

I didn't say anything. He knows so little of what has happened on our planet. If he knew he might not ask any more questions about his daughter's life. There was little chance that she would ever visit them. This trip is not a vacation for me.

"Now I have a question for you," I tell him. "Is there a way to know if someone is in love with you?"

Fred flinched. "You've found someone?"

"Yes, I think so."

Fred looked up at me, sorrow in his eyes, then shook his head and left the room.

TONIA

Another swimming lesson with Branko. He is learning. He actually was able to kick and move forward a few yards today. He was so happy I thought he would explode.

He seems to enjoy the water in a way I've only seen in small children. He can't get enough of it on his body. He is always playing in the lake, splashing me, going under. For someone who nearly drowned in this lake, he is awfully comfortable in it.

When we were done with the lesson, he asked if he could walk me home. "I would like to meet your family," he said.

"Well, there's just me and my little brother. And of course my mom and dad."

"How old is your brother?"

"He's only four. My parents thought another kid might help their marriage."

"Did it?"

"We have yet to see."

He pulled a shirt on over his head and his curly hair sprang up and framed his face. I felt the urge to push it back, to straighten his shirt. But instead I just checked myself out, made sure I had buttoned my shirt correctly. I felt a little goofy around him.

We started walking down the road toward my house. He asked me questions about school. It was nice to walk with a boy who was so tall. He almost made me feel small. He seemed to be shortening his steps so I could keep up with him.

"Are you a runner?" I asked him.

"I run. It's a way we use to get around where I come from."

"Oh, you don't have a car?"

He shrugged his shoulders. "Not many people do. So I run."

"Is it hard to live in your country?"

He didn't say anything for a few steps. Then he said, "It is what I know. I am used to it."

"Would you like to stay here?"

"That is not possible." He had started walking faster. "There's no reason for me to even think about it."

I reached out to slow him down and he grabbed my hand. "I'm sorry. I shouldn't have said that. I didn't mean that your country wasn't a good place to live."

He stopped, still holding on tightly to my hand, and looked down at me very intently. "You can say whatever you want. Don't worry. You won't hurt my feelings. There is a part of me that would like to stay here. But I cannot, so it is easier for me not to think about it."

He started walking again, and he continued to hold my hand. It felt good to be linked like that with him. I felt an energy coming through our hands. I had never walked holding hands with a boy before. Neither of us said anything for a block. We walked next to each other and our hands swung between us, like a bridge between two mountain peaks.

"There's my house." I pointed. I felt awkward with so much silence.

"Oh, good. Now I know where you live. When I go by here, I will know you might be in there."

Buzz was riding his bike with training wheels down the driveway. "There's my little brother."

"He doesn't really look like you."

"I know. He resembles my father."

"You are better-looking. You have such lovely dark hair." Branko turned toward me.

"I take after my mother in coloring, but unfortunately I am my father's size. Mom's a real beauty. You'll see. I'm too big and kind of clunky."

"You are not too big," he said to me. He tipped my head up. "I don't know what clunky means, but you are the most beautiful woman I've ever seen." He said this while staring right into my eyes.

I felt something melt in me then.

I was not embarrassed. Surprised, yes. No one had ever said I was beautiful before. But he was so sure of himself when he spoke that he made me feel like I deserved his praise. "Thank you" was all I could think to say back to him.

My mom stuck her head out the window. "You kids want to come in for a snack?"

As we walked into the house, I introduced Branko to

my mother. He stopped and took her hand. "I am so glad to meet the mother of Tonia."

She smiled and said, "You can call me Lia."

Mom had a plate of brownies on the table and some lemonade. Buzzie grabbed a brownie and went running around the kitchen with it, making airplane noises. Branko watched him and then looked at me. "What is he doing?"

"He's just excited. He always acts like a goof when you give him food."

We sat down at the table and Branko took a brownie. He ate a bite rather slowly and then he took another bite. "This is very good, this brownie."

"Thank you."

He looked over at my mother and said, "Lia, you are a very small woman and yet you had such a big girl. Was that difficult?"

Mom stared at him, then she said, "Well, she wasn't so big when she was a baby."

"Oh, yes, I see," he said.

I showed Branko the house. I even showed him my room. It wasn't too messy. He was interested in everything. He even wanted to look into my closet. "So these are all your clothes?"

I realized that people in Romania might not have as many clothes as we do. Maybe he thought I was frivolous for my full closet so I answered, "Yes, but I plan to give away some to the Goodwill."

Then we went out to the backyard and lounged on the grass. I showed him how to make a grass whistle. At first he couldn't do it at all, but then he did manage to get a small squeak out of it.

"I should go now," he said. "But can I see you tonight?"

"Sure. That'd be great."

"I will come after supper but before the sun goes away. We could go for a walk?"

"That sounds nice."

"He's an awfully big boy," Mom said after Branko left.

"Yes, he is," I agreed.

"He's rather odd-looking," she went on. "And he asks some peculiar questions."

"Mom, you don't have to like him, but I like him just the way he is." I walked away. As those words came out of my mouth, I realized how true they were.

BRANKO

I ate dinner quickly with Martha and Fred. We didn't talk much. I didn't take it personally. I just knew they were very unhappy about their daughter. I think they thought I would provide a strong connection to her, but it hadn't worked out that way. I had told them very little about her life, only as much as I thought they could bear.

I left the house and walked over to Tonia's house. I stood in the shadow of a tree and watched their house for a while before I approached it. I liked the feeling of being near her. The sun was fading from the sky, leaving the clouds as pink as small roses. The blue grew deep and a first star shone through it, not far from where my home is.

Tonia came to the door and looked down the street. When she turned my way, I waved and walked toward her.

"We should go for our walk. It's going to get dark soon," she said.

"I like to walk in the dark."

She stepped down on the front steps. "I do too." She turned back to the house and yelled in, "I'll be back later, Mom."

As she came down the steps, my heart spun in my chest. She looked lovely in the twilight. Her dark hair around her face. Her eyes smiling back at me. I took her hand and she squeezed mine. We started to walk.

"So, Tonia, do you have a boyfriend at school?"

"No," she said, laughing.

"I can't believe it. I would think they would be lined up for you. Have you had a boyfriend?"

She didn't say anything for a moment, then she confessed, "Not really. I went to the roller rink with a boy in seventh grade, but I don't think that counts."

We walked for a while in silence, then she asked, "What about you? Do you have a girlfriend back home?"

I looked up at the sky for a second, then shook my head. "No, I have never had a girlfriend. It is rather hard where I come from."

"Oh," she said, and I knew she wanted to ask me more, but she didn't.

"Could I be your boyfriend?" I asked her.

She stopped walking and turned toward me. "I would like that." She tilted her head back up so she was looking at me. Her eyes softened and her mouth opened slightly. I knew what to do because I had seen it on TV. I lowered my mouth to hers and rubbed. It felt fantastic. She rubbed her lips over mine and then her tongue slipped out and she licked me. I was so surprised, I pulled back.

"I didn't know about that part," I told her.

She looked puzzled.

"The tongue coming in."

"You didn't like it?" she asked.

"Oh, no. I liked it very much, this kissing. I just have never done it before. But you know how to do it?"

"At parties. You learn this stuff."

"Would you teach me more?" I asked.

She pulled me along and we started walking again. "Yes, but not here," she said. "Not in the middle of the street. Let's walk down to the lake."

"Oh, that's a good idea. I like to go there at night. It is so calm and peaceful, the water catches the reflection of the stars."

So we walked for a while and talked, just like in my daydream. She told me about school and about her family. She asked me questions and I did the best I could to answer them. I told her some about Romania but tried not to talk too much, so I wouldn't make any mistakes. When she asked me about my family, I told her the truth.

"My father is a teacher. He is a well-respected man. I have two brothers and they are older than me. One works in law and the other is a scientist. But my mother died when I was very young. She caught a disease that was going around and died suddenly." I didn't tell Tonia that within that year every female on our planet had died.

"Do you miss her?"

"I was only two. I hardly knew her. But yet, I miss her a great deal. I miss having a mother. You are very lucky to have such a nice and beautiful mother."

"I think I am. My mother can be difficult. She is very volatile. Dad compares her to a chemical reaction. But she makes life interesting."

By the time we got to the lake, it was very dark. There was one light on the beach, but we went to the opposite side and sat on the grass under a tree. I touched Tonia's face. She sat quiet and let me. I ran my hand down her hair, I felt her earlobes, I stroked her throat. Then I asked her, "Could we do some more kissing?"

She started to laugh, like a soft wind I heard the sound in my ears. "You are so funny sometimes," she said. "The way you say things."

"I don't always talk very well. I try to say the right words, but I don't always know them."

"You do very well." She whispered in my ear and then she kissed me there. I heard it like a small explosion.

We kissed for quite a while. She showed me all the exploration you could do while kissing. It was much more than I had ever seen on TV. Then I rubbed my nose on her nose and I felt her shiver. "Are you cold?" I asked.

"No. But I like the nose rub."

"That's something we do where I come from." I had seen pictures of it growing up. I had always wanted to try it.

"I knew Eskimos did it, but I didn't know it happened in any other cultures."

Then we looked up at the sky together. She asked me, "Would you ever like to go up there, into outer space?"

I didn't know what to say. I felt like she was reading my mind. "Yes," I finally said, "I think it would be exciting."

"Yes, exciting and scary. I look at the stars spread out like that and sometimes it makes me feel so lonely. Like we are all so far away. Beatrice, my friend, you met her, anyway, she believes in life on other planets. I'm not so sure. I guess I wouldn't say it was impossible."

I was glad that Beatrice was her friend. It might help to have Beatrice on my side. "Beatrice seems like she is very smart."

"Yes, she's called an egghead. Super-brainy. She wants to be an astronomer when she graduates."

"What do you want to be?" I asked.

She turned next to me and rolled closer. "I'm not sure. I've got lots of ideas. I'd like to do something creative, maybe write, maybe paint."

"Do you want to have children?" I held my breath as I waited for her to answer.

"I think so," she said. "Not right away. I'd like to be older, have a career established. Not like my mom, who had me right out of high school. What about you?"

"I would like to have a child more than anything else in the world, in the universe." Finally, I was able to tell her the complete truth.

Beatrice and I lounged on her couch. It was a lovely day outside, but we lay stretched out in the cool darkness of her living room and talked. We hadn't seen each other for a few days, which was very unusual for us. She had been busy with Walter and I with Branko. We had lots to talk about.

She had made a huge bowl of popcorn with plenty of butter and salt. It sat on the floor between us and we would lower a hand into it and then nibble away at it like cats lapping up milk.

"So are you really in love?" I asked her.

"I am," she said. "There's no doubt about it."

There never is much doubt in Beatrice's life. She is very certain about what she believes in. She stopped going to church with her parents when she was nine. She told the pastor she didn't believe in a male god. She refused to say the pledge of allegiance in sixth grade, said it infringed on her civil rights. It was interesting to watch her bring this certainty to her romance.

"Does Walter feel the same way about you?" I asked, wondering what she'd say.

Without any hesitation, she said, "I think he feels stronger about me than I do about him, and that's saying a lot."

I sunk my hand into the popcorn bowl and pulled out a handful.

"How about you?" she asked.

"I think so."

"That was quick."

She knows me so well. I had to explain. "I guess it was. But I've been giving him swimming lessons. We've been together every day since we met."

"That's the way it was with Walter and me. But then we were at camp and so we had to see each other every day. It's not quite as easy now. He can't always get the car and I can almost never get it. But we talk on the phone every day. For hours. Thank god my parents are gone so much or they'd be having a cow."

"So have you guys messed around much?"

Beatrice sat up and looked at me. Her eyes grew wide and round behind her glasses. "What do you mean?"

I sat up too. "You know, kissed and stuff."

"Well, we've kissed. That's for sure. But not too much stuff, if I know what you mean. Why? What have you done with Branko?"

"Oh, we've just kissed. Do you know, I don't think he'd ever kissed before. For sure he never French-kissed before. He actually asked me to teach him."

"Isn't that sweet," Beatrice said, but a slight look of disdain played on her face.

"He is a very quick learner." I remembered his kisses and a little spark ran through me. "But sometimes I feel like he's never been anyplace before. Like he lived in a convent or went to an all-boys school. His mom died when he was very young and he has only brothers in his family. Maybe he's just never been around women much."

"That could be. Some of those Slavic countries can be more protective of their women."

"So how do you feel about slow dancing these days?" I asked Beatrice. That was the phrase she had coined for going all the way. We had talked about sex a fair amount, even if we had had no firsthand knowledge of it. Now that we actually had boyfriends, I felt a little shy bringing it up.

"I'm not in a rush," she said. "Walter says he's feeling very satisfied with what we're doing. To tell you the truth, I think he's just more nervous than I am about that kind of stuff."

"Branko's leaving soon." We were down to the bottom of the popcorn bowl. Only the dud studs, hard kernels that didn't pop, were left.

"That's horrible."

I had to tell her my worst fear. Even saying it was hard for me. "I might never see him again."

"Oh, come on. He'll be back, or you could go over there and visit."

I shrugged my shoulders. "I don't know. You say those things, but then life happens. I have to finish school. He'll go to college or get a job. This might be it for us." I paused, then I went on. "And there's something different about Branko. I have a feeling I don't know the whole story of why he's here this summer."

"I know what you mean. He does seem different. Very foreign. Definitely another species." She sighed. "Seems so unfair. You just get a boyfriend and he leaves. You've been waiting a long time."

I turned toward her. "What would you do if you were really in love with someone, like Walter, and then he had to leave? Would you think of going with him? Would you even consider it?"

"Huh. Go to Romania? I don't think so."

"My mom was almost married when she was my age."

"What would you do in Romania?"

"I don't know. Learn Romanian. Go to college. Help the country. You know, I think they are very poor there. Whenever Branko talks about his home, he gets a sad look on his face. He doesn't have a car there. Never learned how to swim. I think he's going to miss a lot from here."

Beatrice poked me. "Especially you."

BRANKO

Walter taught me how to play chess. He came over to Fred and Martha's and brought a chessboard with him and all the pieces. I had only seen him the one time on the beach and I stared at him. He was such a small man. His hands were half the size of mine. He wore glasses that made his blue eyes look bigger. His hair on his head was light brown and fluffy, more like an animal's fur than Earth human hair.

We sat down at the dining room table and Walter set up the board. He was very patient. He showed me how to make the moves. Then he let me go first.

"Is it a good thing to go first?" I asked.

He looked surprised. "Usually," he admitted.

I jumped a knight over my pawns. Walter let air out through his mouth. He moved out a pawn. We went back and forth for another several moves.

"You're playing awfully fast," he commented, scratching his head.

"Should I play slower?"

"No, but I thought you said you hadn't played this before."

"I haven't," I told him. "But it does remind me of a game that we play back home. Many more pieces, often more players. Very complicated. This chess is a little easier. Not so much to think about."

Walter looked at me with astonishment in his eyes. "What's the name of that game?"

I realized I shouldn't have mentioned it. I didn't know what to say for a moment. "I don't know the translation. I only know the word in Romanian."

"What's that?" he asked.

Now I was stuck. I didn't want to think too long, so I pulled a name out of the air. "Krakow."

Walter paused for a second, rubbed his chin, and said, "Yeah, I think I've heard of that."

I looked with relief back at the board. I could see clearly the next five moves I needed to make in order to capture his king. I think they called it checkmate. Once I had accomplished that, Walter asked me if I wanted to play another game. I said sure. I thought chess was rather fun, a little simple, but it passed the time. But Walter seemed like he was mad about something. I wondered if everything was all right with him and Beatrice.

"How is Beatrice these days?" I asked him.

The question surprised him. "She's good."

"Are you two going to marry and have children?" I asked.

The pawn he was holding fell out of his hand and bounced on the carpet. "We're a little young."

"I know that the average age of marriage has risen in the United States, but still, many people marry under the age of twenty. You're nearly eighteen, aren't you?"

"Yes, but I want to go to college. I admire Beatrice a

great deal. We are having a wonderful time together this summer, but who knows what will happen next year."

"But that is exactly what I mean. You two look like you are in love. I know how important that is for you Americans. Why not marry and have children? You are both smart and so you will have smart children and this will be good. It will be good for you and good for your country."

Walter just stared at me. I don't know what was possessing me. I was talking too much. I couldn't help it. My heart was full. My head burst with ideas. I needed to talk to someone. Fred didn't want to listen. Martha sniffed at me and turned away. I thought maybe Walter might understand, but it looked like I was scaring him. I decided to turn it into a joke.

"Oh, you know, whatever happens. I was only kidding," I said, and laughed.

Walter spun the pawn in his fingers. "How about you and Tonia? How's that going?"

I could not make a joke out of his question. I simply told him, "I don't know what I would do without her."

☾ TONIA

I have to admit I was nervous. I wanted my father and mother to like Branko. Actually, I wanted more than that. I wanted them to admire him, to think he was good enough for me, to consider buying me a plane ticket to visit him sometime. So this dinner was important to me. But what really made me nervous was wondering how Branko would behave. He was unpredictable. I wanted this dinner to be bordering on normal. My family can stretch quite a ways. Both my parents are their own form of weird. But Branko was also full of surprises.

So I set the table carefully. Mom had made my favorite meal: pork chops, mashed potatoes, and a fruit salad. I made angel food cake for dessert. It was one of my few specialties. My grandmother told me that you always bake well when you really like the dish you are making. I adore angel food cake. Especially with fresh strawberries and whipped cream.

When Branko rang the doorbell, Buzz jumped up from where he was huddled in front of the TV set and ran for the door, screaming that he would answer it. I continued to set the table, wanting to appear as calm as possible. But inside my muscles were jumping. I hadn't seen Branko yesterday and I couldn't believe how much I had missed him. This was not a good sign for the rest of my life. He had mentioned that he was leaving in less than a week.

When Buzz swung open the door, Branko stood in the doorway, as big as ever, with a huge bouquet of flowers in his arms. "Martha let me pick some of the flowers in her garden. I wanted to bring you something." He walked up to me and pushed the flowers into my arms. I didn't know what half of them were, but there were hollyhocks and roses, daisies and gladiolas, snapdragons and petunias. It was a very strange bouquet. "Thank you. They are beautiful."

Branko leaned over and I could tell he was going to kiss me. But I didn't want him to kiss me in front of my family, so I ducked and walked toward the kitchen. "Let me just give these flowers to my mother to put in a vase."

"Martha said they would need some water," he told me.

I nodded and handed them over to my mother. She stared at the flowers and then smiled and said, "I'll see what I can do."

I went out and asked Branko if he wanted to sit down in the living room. He moved toward me again and tried to kiss me. This time I grabbed his neck and whispered in his ear, "Not now."

"What did you tell him?" Buzz asked.

"Never mind," I said.

"Did you try to kiss her?" Buzz asked Branko.

"Yes, but I think she wants me to wait."

Buzz shrugged his shoulders. "I don't mind. Mom and Dad kiss and it's okay with me."

I wrapped my arms around Buzz's neck and pulled

him into the living room with us. "I'm so glad we have your permission. Now my life is complete."

"Do you play basketball?" Buzz asked Branko.

"No, but I learned how to play chess yesterday."

Branko sat down on the couch and Buzz sat next to him. The two of them sitting next to each other made Branko appear even bigger than usual. I felt a strong rush of emotion for both of them.

"Oh, I can play Nintendo. But my parents don't want me to."

"Why not?" Branko asked.

"They say it eats away at your brain."

"That would be bad," Branko said seriously.

"I guess so. But a lot of my friends play it and they still have all their brains."

"You sure are a little jabbermouth," I said to Buzz.

"Well, you told me to be nice to him."

I laughed.

"Do you want to see my rock collection?" Buzz asked him.

"Buzzy, leave him be."

"I'd love to see it." They both stood up and Buzz took Branko's hand to lead him upstairs to his bedroom. The gesture made me realize that Buzz probably wishes he had an older brother sometimes.

When they came back down, dinner was ready. Dad was seated at the head of the table and Mom was bringing in the serving dishes from the kitchen. I told Branko to take the chair between Dad and me.

"But I want him to sit next to me," Buzz whined.

Branko looked at me to tell him what to do.

"Oh, I guess he can sit by you." I gave up. I didn't want Buzz whining all through dinner. Besides, Dad had given me permission to take the car for a while after dinner, so I would have plenty of time to sit next to Branko.

My dad stood up and shook hands with Branko. "It's nice to meet you, son. I've never met anyone from Romania before."

"Not many people here have," Branko said.

Dad laughed. "I'm sure you're right. We weren't on too friendly terms for quite a while."

We all sat down and Mom started passing the dishes around. I was amazed at how much food Branko put on his plate, except he didn't take any pork chops. Maybe he didn't eat meat. I was glad Mom had made big portions of everything.

"How did you happen to get sent over to the States for the summer? Most students your age come for the school year."

"I was sent here to practice my English. It will help me get a job."

"And what is your connection with the family you are staying with?"

"They have relatives in my country. Friends of my father."

When I heard that something inside me tingled. A

connection to Branko even after he was gone. Other people went to his country. Maybe I could too.

My father wiped his mouth with his napkin and then asked, "What does your father do for a living?"

"He teaches at the university."

"What field is he in?"

"Field." Branko looked confused. "I don't know this word."

"What does he teach?"

"Oh, genetics."

I felt proud of Branko. He came from an intelligent family. This would impress my father.

The dinner was going so nicely. Buzz was eating his food without spilling any on his clothes. He was watching every move Branko made and then copying him. Branko finished all his food before anyone else. My mother offered him more to eat. He said he was fine.

"But there is dessert. Tonia made it especially for you."

"Well, anything Tonia made I will like. I know it already." He looked across the table and smiled at me.

I was so happy. A real success. I stood up and was going into the kitchen to serve the cake when I heard Branko ask my father, "Sir, how is your marriage going? Are you still seeing someone else?"

I thought of walking out the back door and not stopping.

☾ BRANKO

Tonia told me in no uncertain terms that I had asked the wrong question at the dinner table. She tried to be mad at me, but it didn't work. For one thing she was buried deep in my arms and for another she was laughing.

When I had asked if Tonia's father was still seeing someone else, there was a horrible silence at the table. Then everyone started talking at once. Her mother stood up, her father threw down his napkin, Tonia ran back and forth between them. Finally, they all calmed down and it turned out that her father wasn't seeing anyone else and had no idea that her mother thought he was. They straightened it all out and when we left, Tonia's parents had their arms around each other. I felt I was rather a hero.

In the car Tonia explained that her mother often needed some excitement in her life and if it wasn't there, she created it. I puzzled over this, but decided there were some things about these people I would not understand.

Tonia asked me if I wanted to drive out to the St. Croix River. Light still remained in the sky and we parked near the river. The water flowed below us. The trees shone green in the last light of the sun. Tonia turned the car off, but left the radio on. She played some music she called classical and it sounded like a river moving. We put the seats back and got very close to each other. I liked this thing called "parking." The car was a room on wheels.

We kissed a bit and then we talked. We watched the sun set. We saw the moon as it rose, big and white as a plate in the sky. Where I come from there are no moons and this one surprised me every night when it appeared in the sky. Tonia told me a lot more about her family, how her parents had met, how worried she had been that they might leave each other.

"I wouldn't want to have to choose between them," she said. "But pretty soon I'll be on my own. They can do what they want."

She asked me when I was going back home. I told her that it was soon. We both stayed silent for a while. I didn't want to ask her to come with me. It felt like it was too soon to bring that up. And yet we didn't have much time left.

"Will we be able to talk on the phone?" she asked.

"My family doesn't have a phone," I told her.

"Your father is a professor and you don't have a phone?"

"He has a phone at his office."

"Great. You can go there and I'll call you."

"We'll see."

Her voice grew faint. "What do you mean, 'we'll see'?"

"Tonia, I don't want to talk about leaving right now. I don't want to think about it. I'm here. Let's enjoy it."

Mainly we talked, but every once in a while we would

have to kiss some more, almost as if we were checking to see if the other person was still there in the dark. I wanted to do more than just kiss. They had taught us about sex at the classes I had taken. It was not forbidden, but they stressed over and over again that it must be a welcome act by the female.

Kissing Tonia felt like learning how to swim. The water was warm, my arms were strong, but I felt like there might be some hidden danger. I didn't want to get in over my head. So I followed Tonia. I did what she did. If she pulled back, I let go. If she moved toward me, I met her halfway.

But there were times when I wanted to go charging into the water, when I wanted to drown in her.

☾ TONIA

When I crawled out of bed this morning, my mother was waiting for me at the counter in the kitchen with this look on her face. It was what I called her "you have really done it now" look. I was worried that now that she wasn't obsessing about Dad she would focus on me.

"What?" I asked, as I poured myself a bowl of Grape-Nuts and sloshed milk all over it.

"Do you know what time it is?" she asked.

I didn't, but I knew I was about to find out. I shook my head no. I didn't want to open my mouth as I was eating. When Mom was in this mood, she would take the opportunity to yell about anything.

"It is past noon."

I leaned back in my chair at the counter. "Oh, no. I was supposed to meet Branko at the beach."

"He's already stopped by and I told him that you wouldn't be seeing him for a while."

"You did what?" I stood up so fast, the chair I had been sitting in flew over backward.

"You are grounded. Your father and I talked it over last night when you weren't home at two o'clock in the morning with no phone call, and we agreed that you would be grounded."

"Where's Dad?"

"He's golfing."

"Are you guys mad at me because I told Branko that you thought Dad was seeing someone else?"

"No, not particularly." She ran her hands over her hair, which was perfect. She was probably just nervous. She was never very good at being the disciplinary mom.

"But you've never grounded me."

"You've never behaved like this before."

"Mom, I'm seventeen years old. I could get married if I wanted to. I could drop out of school. How can you ground me?"

"You live in this house. We make the rules, not you."

I picked up the chair and sat back down in it. "Mom, you don't understand."

"That's the problem, Tonia, I do. Remember, I met your father at your age."

I stared at her and she stared back. My mother is a very stubborn woman. "But, Mom, Branko won't be here much longer. I have to see him. This is it for us."

"Well, that's another reason why it might be a good idea for you to slow down. Take a couple days off. He seems like a nice guy, quite foreign, but nice. You two should work on being friends. After all, he is leaving."

"Mom, I finally have a boyfriend and now you're telling me I can't see him. I might never have another boyfriend in my whole life."

"I highly doubt that."

"I'm not the kind of girl that guys like. I'm too big and too something. Maybe opinionated."

"That will change. Boys your age are still a little immature."

Something in me snapped. I was tired of hearing my mom tell me I was a late bloomer, that men would appreciate me more as they got older. I was seventeen. It felt plenty old to me. I slapped my spoon into my bowl and saw drops of milk fly across the counter and hit my mother in the face. I stood up and screamed at her, "Branko likes me. He more than likes me. He loves me. He's not like anybody else. He's from a different place, a different planet. I'm never going to find anyone like him again."

BRANKO

I was forbidden from seeing Tonia. The world changed color. The sun was black, the clouds covered all the sky. I didn't know what to do with myself. Where before there didn't seem to be enough hours in the day, now the minutes marched so very slowly they felt like hours. I sat on the rug in the living room at Martha and Fred's house. I stared at the fibers and thought of pulling them out, one by one.

Then I decided to go see Beatrice. She would tell me what to do.

When Beatrice came to her door, she was surprised to see me. I explained what had happened to Tonia. She told me that Walter had gone to visit his grandparents. She seemed happy to talk to me.

We sat down on the front steps. I liked sitting next to Beatrice better than standing, that way her head wasn't so much lower than mine.

Beatrice asked me, "What are you going to do about Tonia?"

"I can't live like this. I must see her." My hands raised up in the air in front of me as if they were clutching at something.

"You guys don't have much time left, do you?"

"No," I admitted, shaking my head.

"Is Tonia going to visit you back in Romania?"

"It's complicated," I said.

"What is it like—where you live?"

I didn't really want to talk about my home at that moment. "It's not like here. It's so far away. Cold, dry, people are poor. What do you want me to say?"

Beatrice squinted her eyes at me. "Are you really from Romania?"

I didn't say anything.

"You don't look like a Romanian. You're so big and your skin is so smooth." She stopped and thought for a moment.

"Maybe you are from Transylvania." When she said this her voice changed and she talked funny. Also she showed me her teeth.

"Close, but I am not from there."

"You can tell me," she assured me.

"All I want is help to see Tonia. How can I get to see Tonia? Can you go talk to her and find out what's going on? I'm afraid if I go back over there, her mother will get mad. I don't want to make things bad for Tonia at home. That's not my intention."

Beatrice stared at me.

"You will help me, won't you?"

"Yes. But you must promise me that you will never do anything to hurt Tonia."

"That is an easy promise to make."

☽ TONIA

I lay on my bed and listened to my heart beat. If you put your hand on your neck, it sounds like your heart is in your head. I decided my heart *was* in my head. I wasn't thinking anymore. I was simply feeling. Somehow Branko had become part of my body and I felt like I was cut in two now that I couldn't see him. It was not a pleasant feeling. I thought back to the time, only a few weeks ago, when I hadn't known any of this.

Someone pounded on my door and I told them to go away.

"Tonia, it's me."

At the sound of Beatrice's voice, I sat bolt upright and then bounced off my bed and landed on my feet. I pulled the door open and stared at her. "Beatrice . . ."

"I know. I know. He came over to my house. He's pretty upset."

I yanked her into my room and slammed the door. "He is?"

"Of course. What do you expect? He doesn't know what to do without you."

"Did he say that?"

"He doesn't have to. He looks like a fish out of water."

"Oh, god, Beatrice. Don't do this to me."

"Hey, listen, I'm serious. Now that we're both in love, I know how you feel and vice versa. I think it was very good planning that we both fell in love at the same time."

Beatrice was so practical. Even in love. She couldn't help it. It was one of those qualities about her that I loved and that also irked me.

"So what should I do?"

"Sneak out," she whispered back to me.

"Really?"

"I don't think you have time to waste trying to convince your parents of anything. Plus, you're such a good kid that they will never suspect you would do such a thing."

"Like tonight?"

"Precisely."

"Could you help me set it up?"

"Absolutely. I told Branko I'd bring back a message to him. He's sitting on my front steps as we speak."

Somehow knowing where he was made him seem closer to me.

"But I have to tell you something." She sat down on the edge of my bed and patted it.

I sat down next to her. "What?"

"I think Branko is not who he claims to be."

This surprised me.

"You know Walter played chess with him the other day and Branko beat Walter two out of three. Yet Branko said he had never played chess before. He mentioned some game that was even harder than chess. Walter said the only game he knows of like that is Go and it's a

Japanese game. This got Walter to thinking. You know Branko really doesn't like to talk about Romania. He won't say much about it. Also, he doesn't have the normal stature of a Romanian. We don't think he's from Romania."

"You don't?" This had never occured to me.

"No. We actually think there's a very good chance he's an alien."

"You mean like an illegal alien?"

"No, like from another planet."

I stared at her. She still looked like Beatrice, my best friend. Then I burst out laughing. I laughed so hard I started to choke. I grabbed my pillow and held it over my face so my mom wouldn't hear. When I finally came up for air, Beatrice glared at me.

"Are you done?" she asked.

I nodded my head, not wanting to try to speak yet.

"His head is shaped rather oddly, his skin seems smoother than usual, his eyes are a very strange color, and his hair is an unusual texture."

She was right about all those characteristics. I had noticed them all, but hadn't thought much more about them.

"Has he told you much about his life?"

"Only a little," I admitted.

"Have you ever heard him speak Romanian?" she asked.

"Well, maybe. When I rescued him he said something

I didn't understand." I remembered that odd word, more like a sound. "Now that you mention it, the sound he made was quite peculiar. Almost like birdsong."

She gave a little smile and then grew determined. "If I help you do this with Branko, help you meet him tonight, then you need to find out more about him. Is that a deal?"

I didn't like the idea of trying to weasel information out of Branko for Beatrice, but I was curious myself. "I will try."

"Listen, if nothing else works, ask him straight out. Actually I asked him today if he really was from Romania."

"You did? What did he say?"

"He didn't say anything. He didn't deny it or say he was. Now, I think that's very strange behavior."

I felt like I wanted to be by myself to think about all of this. But I needed to set up arrangements for that night. "So about tonight," I started.

"What time do your parents go to sleep?"

"They're usually in bed by eleven."

"Okay, I think simple is best. Branko knows where your bedroom is, doesn't he?"

"Yes."

"I'll tell him to throw a pebble at your window around midnight. How does that sound?"

"How am I going to get out of my room?"

"Tonia, you need to figure some of this out. How

about that old trellis? Can you use that to climb down?"

"I'll see."

Beatrice stood up to go. "So how far have you guys gone? Have you done the slow dance?"

"No."

"Us either. I wonder who will be first."

BRANKO

For three long hours I sat in a big shrub right by Tonia's house. One by one the lights in the house went out. Finally it was completely dark. Even Tonia's room. Which made me wonder if she was really waiting for me. Maybe she fell asleep. I had borrowed Fred's watch so I would know when it was twelve o'clock. The dial shone a faint green glow and I could see the big hand was only a few minutes away from twelve. I couldn't wait any longer. I moved away from the house and threw the small stone that I'd clutched in my hand for three hours. I tried to do it gently because I didn't want to break the window. I didn't want her to get into any more trouble. I was already so sorry for what I had done to her.

I heard the stone hit the window, a light sound, and then nothing. No light went on. No movement, that I could see, inside. I sat and stared at her window. Then her face appeared like the moon behind glass. I waved up at her, she waved down at me. I walked over to the broken-down trellis and got ready to help her down. She slowly edged the window up and then wedged a big book into it. She turned and her feet came out first, reaching for the top of the trellis.

Suddenly, I was so afraid. The trellis looked too fragile. Tonia would not be able to reach it. I was sure she was going to fall and hurt herself. Why had I agreed to this? I had promised Beatrice I would do nothing to hurt Tonia and there I was watching her hang precariously from her window. I positioned myself so if she were to fall I could catch her.

Tonia's foot found the top of the trellis. She swung out of the window and down. Her other foot was on the trellis. Her fingers were still gripping the windowsill. I could almost reach her. She let go of the sill and stepped down onto the trellis.

For a moment, she looked like she had made it and then her hands clutched at the side of the house and her foot slipped.

She fell back away from the house. I grabbed her around the thighs as she crashed into my chest. Then I folded and we fell easily to the ground. She had landed on me and I knew she was fine. I rolled with her in my arms and then I was on top of her. I covered her face with kisses. She was laughing soundlessly under me. I was hardly letting her breathe.

I held her face in my hands.

I said, "Tonia, my Tonia."

She whispered in my ear, "Now you have saved me."

☾ TONIA

We went to the beach. We didn't even talk about it. We both just headed that way. It seemed natural. Once we were away from my house, we started laughing and talking. The night was ours. No one else was out on the streets. We were alone in the middle of the town. People slept all around us as we skipped and ran down the streets. It was like a movie. It was like a story. It was my very own life.

Somehow what we had done made us more to each other. We had leaped a barrier. We belonged to each other. No one could keep us apart. That was how I felt.

It was a warm, end-of-the-summer night. Branko wrapped an arm around my neck and we walked close and in step. When we got to the park, we kept on walking until we came right down to the water's edge.

"Do you want to go swimming?" I asked him.

"Now?"

"Sure. Why not? It's warm."

"I don't have my suit."

"We can go skinny-dipping."

"I don't know this."

"We can go swimming with no clothes on."

"Oh," he said. "I like that."

So right there we took our clothes off and made two piles of clothes on the shore. There was a little light from the moon, which was only half full. I was glad because all of a sudden I felt shy.

Branko took my hand and we walked slowly into the water together. As the water moved up my body, I felt cold, then warmed as I stepped into it. When I was up to my waist I leaned forward and dove in. As I came to the surface I heard Branko let out a whoop and he plunged in next to me. A moment later, he was floating on the surface of the water.

"This is the best!" he shouted. "Like animals we swim naked."

"Sshh," I told him.

"Why be quiet?"

"Because we don't want the police to come down here."

"Why would they come?"

"It's against the law to skinny-dip."

He swam up close to me and looked at my face. "No, you are kidding with me."

"I'm not."

"How can such a thing be against the law? There is no one here and if they were here they couldn't see us."

"I know it doesn't make sense, but that's the way it is."

"So we are breaking the law. I like it." He came closer and wrapped his arms around me.

I didn't know what to do. I had never been naked with a man before. My whole body was next to his whole body. Only a thin layer of water separated us.

"Are you cold?" he asked.

"No," I said.

"You seem stiff or something."

"I'm a little nervous."

"About what?"

"You know, being like this with you."

He brought his face close to mine and kissed me gently on the lips. "But it's me, Tonia. It's only me."

"There is no only you."

"I don't understand."

"You are the most dangerous man for me."

"Why?"

"Because of the way I feel about you." I put my hand out and touched his face.

"How do you feel about me?"

"I think we should swim some more." I slipped from his grasp and swam underwater for a few yards.

"Tonia, don't go," he yelled at me.

"You can swim too." I waited for him. He pushed himself off the bottom and started kicking. His hands moved in front of him and he pulled back. The movement he was doing was really the dog paddle, but he was making progress in the water. In a few moments, he was next to me.

"You did it. You can swim." I rubbed the top of his wet head as we both stood on the sandy bottom.

"I owe it all to you, my teacher." He came in close to me again. He put a hand under my chin and tipped my head back. He kissed me and when I closed my eyes, I didn't know where I ended and the water began, where he stopped and I started. We were merging together in the lake. Everything was getting rather slippery.

I pulled back and said, "Let's go to shore. I'm cold."

We both ran out of the water and dried ourselves on Branko's sweatshirt. Then we slipped back into our clothes. The wind had picked up and low clouds scudded across the lake. We found a patch of grass and Branko sat down and I fit in between his legs. He wrapped his arms around me. The world was full of wind and quiet at the same time. I felt like I could feel his heart beating through my body.

"We only have a couple days left," I said.

"I don't want to think."

"Branko, where are you from, exactly?"

I felt him tense against me. "Why?"

"Well, Beatrice was curious."

"Beatrice will always be curious."

"But I need to know if I'm going to stay in touch with you."

"You can't," he said.

"What?" I turned in his arms and crouched in front of him. "Why not?"

"It's too far."

"No place on Earth is too far."

He didn't say anything. He didn't disagree with me.

"Branko, I need to know."

"Tonia, would you come with me to my home?"

"Where?"

Branko turned his face up to the dark sky.

"Branko, are you from another planet?"

He looked at me. "I have been sent here to bring you back with me."

"Why?"

"We need you. We need to repopulate and for that we need more females. They have all died."

I sat back down on the grass and stared at him. The light from the streetlight lit up half his face. He looked very otherworldly at that moment. But I couldn't stand the thought of losing him.

"I don't understand. Are you trying to tell me that you come from someplace else? Not Romania?"

His head tilted forward slightly.

"Look at me." I forced his head so his eyes were staring into mine. His odd-colored eyes. "Tell me what you mean."

"I have come here from another planet."

"Don't tell me that." I pulled away from him.

"I have already said it. I cannot pull the words back."

"Where? Why us? What are you doing here? How are you different from us?"

He opened his shirt, reached up to his nipples, and pulled them off. His bare chest shone in the light.

I stared at him. He had always looked slightly different, but I had gotten used to him. Now all I could see was how alien he looked. Frizzy hair, odd eyes, and a completely bare chest.

He pointed at his chest. "This is one of the ways we are different. There are many other small differences. But the good thing is that we can procreate together."

"Have children?"

"Yes, otherwise our planet will die."

"You want me to go back with you and have children?"

"Yes."

BRANKO

Taking Tonia back to her house was sad. I did not want to be apart from her.

When she climbed up the trellis, I thought of going up after her. I would curl up on the floor at the foot of her bed, like a dog. I would watch over her all through the night. I would be there when she woke up. I would see the light of the sun in her eyes.

She waved from the window. She whispered she would see me the next day. She would tell me then. She would give me the answer about returning with me. She had asked a million questions and I had tried to answer them all. Sometimes she seemed excited, but I felt her shiver in my arms.

I knew it was a difficult decision—to go to another planet. I had made it for my people. She would have to make it only for me. I did not know if that would be reason enough for her.

After she left the window, I went back to my shrub. I curled up next to it. I slept a little. When the sun came up early, I awoke. I felt the cold earth under me and the branches of the shrub scratched me as I sat up. The first thing I thought of was Tonia. I thought, Tonia is sleeping up above me. We might never get a chance to sleep together. I stood up and walked across the lawn, leaving dewy footprints in the grass.

☾ TONIA

My dad is an early riser. When he woke up at six the next morning, I heard him and went down to join him at the breakfast table. He had scrambled the newspaper all around him. The crusts of two pieces of toast had been neatly nibbled around and he was drinking very black coffee.

"Hi, Dad," I said cheerfully.

"What? You're up so early?" he said. "Did you get any sleep last night?"

"Not much," I admitted. "I have to talk to you."

"No," he said, and disappeared behind the paper.

"What do you mean—no?"

"Whatever it is—no."

"That's not fair."

He dropped the paper and smiled at me. "That's the pledge of being a good parent. Never be fair."

"Da-a-a-d."

He looked at me with an open face. My dad has big blue eyes and nice wrinkles that lace the corners of them. He waited for me to speak.

"I know that you and Mom talked and decided I should be grounded because I stayed out too late and didn't call . . . but I've never done anything like that before and Branko is leaving in two days and he's the first boyfriend I ever had, so I'm begging you to change your mind."

"Okay," he said.

"Dad, you're the best."

He smiled. "I must confess it was your mother's idea."

"Thanks."

"You can see him for the next few nights, but don't stay out so late."

"I promise."

"Like you did last night." He dove back into the newspaper.

☾ BRANKO

I can't believe I waited so long to ask her.

The sun is in the middle of the sky.

I won't see Tonia until tonight. She will tell me then. I will know if I have succeeded in my mission. If she comes back home with me, everything will be good. But if she will not come, life will be difficult. Father will do the best he can for me, but I will be in disgrace.

I am lying in the backyard, staring up at the sky. Unlike humans we can stare at the sun. It does not hurt our eyes. I know it makes Martha uncomfortable to see me stare. I have seen her peek out the window three times. But if I stare at the sun I absorb the heat from it.

I leave in less than two days. I will need the warmth and the memory of it to last me through the long ride home.

☽ TONIA

I went over to Beatrice's as soon as I thought there was a chance she might be up. Unfortunately, I caught her still in bed. She is not happy in the morning when she wakes up. Especially if she's woken up. I understand. I have a similar reaction. So I just let her fume. Unable to say whole words, she muttered.

"Beatrice, it's important that we talk. I need you."

Sitting on the edge of her bed, she rubbed her toes together and yawned. This burst of activity exhausted her and she slumped. I nudged her.

"How about I go downstairs and stir up some breakfast for you?"

No response.

"French toast?"

She lifted her head.

"Just the way you like it, extra eggy."

She nodded.

I left the room. I couldn't help her anymore. She would be better on her own.

I know her kitchen almost as well as I know my own. I had the pan hot and the toast ready to go in when she appeared in the doorway. She had tried. A sweatshirt was pulled over her nightgown and she was wearing her bunny slippers.

"Morning," she said.

"Oh, good, you're talking in words now." I plunked the French toast in the pan. I was bursting to tell her everything, but until she was fed it would be impossible. She sat at the dining room table and I brought in the French toast as soon as it was ready. She slathered it with butter. Just as she picked up the syrup and started pouring it over her toast, I had to tell her.

"He is an alien, I think," I told her.

"What?" The word came out like a whoop. She tipped the syrup bottle up too high and a wave of syrup flooded her toast.

"He wants me to go back with him."

"No way." Her eyes drilled into me.

"I know," I said.

"Where? What?" she stammered.

"I don't have all the info."

"Are you even considering?" she asked.

"Well, I'm thinking about it."

"Tonia. I can't believe it."

"But you were the one . . ."

"But this is for real."

We both sat there staring at her French toast. I had ruined the toast for her. She poked it with her fork. The toast was actually floating in the syrup. I went and got her another plate. Carefully she transferred both pieces of toast to the new plate after letting them drip for a few moments over the old plate.

When the French toast had been safely moved, I said,

"What am I going to do?"

She cut her toast into small square pieces. It reassured me to see that she hadn't been thrown off her feed by this news. Maybe it wasn't so odd after all.

"That is the question," she remarked.

"This is so unfair. You've got a regular boyfriend who is an American and lives nearby. You can afford to get mad at him and everything. He's not going anyplace. Branko is leaving tomorrow. If I don't go with him, I'll never see him again."

"Do you have any idea what you're getting into? Do the people of his planet want aliens?" she screamed, and put down her fork. "You would be an alien. You would be a creature from outer space to them."

"Don't go and get metaphysical on me. No. In answer to your question I have no idea what I would be getting into. The only thing I know is that they need more women on their planet."

Beatrice started on her second piece of toast. "This is pretty sweet," she commented.

"I imagine."

She waved her fork at me. "You need more information. You can't make a decision based on the little you know. It is your job to get all you can get out of Branko before you give him a definite answer."

"I'll never meet anyone like Branko again. In my whole life."

"That's for sure."

⊙ ˚ ◦ ☽ BRANKO

This Tonia, she is a smart woman. When I walked over to her house, she was sitting on the front steps with a blanket in her lap. She stared at me as I walked up to her. She stared at me like I was a stranger, someone she had never seen before. Actually, she stared at me as if I were from another planet. Maybe she was seeing me for the first time. I put my hand on her cheek and she leaned into me.

Standing up suddenly, she dangled keys in front of my face. "My parents are being very understanding. I told them you are leaving tomorrow night and they let us have the car. I guess they think we can't get in any trouble." She paused and stared at me with a kind of hunger in her eyes. "Let's prove them wrong."

She walked toward the car and I followed her.

I slid into the passenger seat and she started the car. Tapping her on the shoulder, I asked her if she had decided.

"I need to know more."

"Okay." I had been prepared for this.

"You want to go for a drive on the freeway?"

"Sure."

"I feel like going fast."

We drove down a street called 36 until it intersected with the very large freeway called 694. Tonia explained to me that it was the loop route around the Twin Cities.

Tonia manuevered the car in and around other vehicles. I wasn't scared. I found it exciting.

"What do you want to know?" I asked her.

"Tell me what happened to the women."

I stared at the fading sky. "It started when I was little. I don't really remember my mother. Maybe I have an early image of her. A sense of love. A feeling of warmth. But then, in one year, all the women on our planet died of a disease that only affected them. None of the men got it. They had to stand by and watch their women die, unable to do anything. Then my planet, home, we call it, was a planet of men. No babies. No life. At least my father was lucky. He had had three boys. So his wife died, but no children. The scientists on our planet started to search the planets in our solar system, and about five years ago they discovered your planet and determined that we could mate. So that's what has happened."

"You have already taken Earth women back to your planet?"

"Yes." I had been instructed to answer her questons, but to the point. Not add any information to them. There was so much she would not think to ask.

"So now you have babies on your planet?"

"Yes, we do. When I left there were four hundred and thirty-four new babies. Two hundred and five are baby girls. They are very special to us. There are two billion men on my planet. So we still need more women."

"I guess. How did you get selected to come to Earth?"

"My father is important. I was chosen because I have good genes."

"Why don't you just take women? Come and steal them?"

"That is not our way. We don't believe in violence. The women we bring back to our planet are treated very well. After all, we worship them. But it is up to them to decide that this is right for them." I paused and then continued, trying to keep my voice constant and soothing. "My planet is a remarkable place. We have no violence, no war. When there were women among us, they were our equals. Now they are above us, because we have so few. People live in harmony. Yet my planet is going to come close to dying, even with the new women we are bringing in. For ten years we have been losing older men and having no children to replace them. Our population is shrinking very fast. We hope the infrastructure of the whole civilization won't collapse. It already took a beating when half our population died." I had saved the best for last. "We live longer than you. We have learned how to live to be over a hundred and fifty. Long lives lead to some wisdom."

"It sounds amazing."

"Yes, and more."

"Will I get to stay with you?"

"Yes. But I should put it, I get to stay with you."

"I have to have babies, don't I?"

I knew how Tonia felt about that.

"Yes. That would be good."

"I would be helping to save your planet, yes?"

"Absolutely."

"Could I go to school, have a job?"

"There would be no need."

"For me, there would be a need. I am a smart woman and I would want to do something."

I said nothing. It was best not to tell her how confined her life would be.

She pulled off the freeway onto an exit ramp and circled back around. "I still need to think."

"Of course."

"Do you want to go to the lake?"

"Of course."

We didn't talk much on the way to the lake. Tonia reached over and held my hand. It was such a simple act and yet I felt like it meant everything. It meant she loved me. It meant she was truly thinking about coming home with me. When our hands touched we were like one person. I could feel the blood flowing through her wrist.

When we got to the lake, I was nervous. She was being so quiet. I didn't want to push her. We sat next to each other in the quiet car. No one was on the beach.

"Don't you want to kiss me?" she asked.

"Well, I do. But I don't want to seem like I'm pushing you."

She leaned toward me and we kissed. Electricity ran along my lips where she touched me. A slight moan escaped from my mouth.

"I brought a blanket," she said. "We could go and spread it out on the grass. It isn't too cold outside."

"I would like that," I said.

We found a patch of grass near a tree and stretched the blanket out. The stars blanketed the sky. The moon wasn't up yet so they shone very brightly. I could hear the water hit the shore like a heartbeat. I would miss the water.

We sat down next to each other. Tonia turned to me and said, "I'd like you to do something for me. When I rescued you when you were drowning, you said something to me. It sounded like a bird sound. Was that your language? Would you talk to me in your language?"

I nodded and started out softly. Our language was so different from Earth language. We used a much larger range of tones. The closest human language came to it was singing. In my language, singing to her, I told her everything. How much I wanted her to come with me, how scared I was for her, how hard it would be. Everything I had been unable to tell her I poured out to her in my own tongue.

She sat with her head bent low toward her knees. I could tell she was listening but I couldn't see her face. The last thing I said to her in my home language was "Tonia, I love you."

She lifted her face when I was done and I saw it was wet with tears. But there was a slight laugh in her voice when she said, "I almost feel like I understood the last thing you said to me." Then she put her arms around me and hugged me. "I don't know if I could ever learn to talk like that."

"You could," I told her. "Others have."

"Branko," she whispered into my shoulder. "I want you."

I held her without breathing. I wasn't sure I understood what she meant. I didn't want to ask her.

Then I felt her hand slide inside my pants.

No language was needed. As with swimming, she taught me. She was the water. She was the waves. I swam. With her strong arms around me, I swam.

When she dropped me off at my house, she said she would go with me. I told her to meet me at six o'clock in the evening at my house. She asked if she should bring anything.

"No," I told her. "You will never want for anything again. It will all be provided for you. You are doing a great thing for my people."

☾ TONIA

I knew I would go when I heard him talk in his language. It pulled me from the center of my belly. I yearned to be where people spoke like that, singing the words as if they explained everything.

But I must admit that when he began speaking of his planet, I was envious. They sounded so much further along in evolution than us. Peace, harmony, equality. What more could a woman want?

I knew in Branko I had found my partner. I knew, even though I didn't understand the words, that when he sang to me, it was of love.

I knew I would go with him.

I woke up early the next morning, too excited to sleep late. I had dreamed I was falling. These dreams came to me from time to time. Sometimes I was falling off a cliff, sometimes down a well. But this time, when I thought about it, when I remembered my dream after waking, I realized I was hurtling through space.

I climbed out of bed at seven o'clock and found my mother puttering around in the kitchen. Dad had left early for a breakfast meeting and she seemed quite happy with herself. I was so glad they were getting along again. It would make leaving easier.

But I realized I didn't want to talk to my mother right

now. What if she pried something out of me?

When I sat down, she asked me if I wanted a piece of toast.

"Yes," I said. "Thanks, Mom."

She didn't ask me anything else. Just set a piece of toast on a plate in front of me and went about her own business.

Finally, she asked, "Are you seeing Branko tonight?"

When I thought of what I was doing tonight, I found it hard to answer her. I managed to say, "Yes."

"He kind of grows on you, doesn't he?" she asked cheerily.

I said, "Yes," one more time and stood up and left the table.

☽ BRANKO

I was so happy, I didn't sleep all night. I stared out the window at the stars, wondering where the transportation ship was. Soon it would be here. Now that Tonia had said yes, I wanted to go home.

I had done what I was sent here to do. I had found a female and she was coming home with me. My father would be so proud of me. And I would have the magic of Tonia in my life forever.

I cleaned my room. I pulled the sheets off the bed and washed them for Martha. I packed my clothes. I would bring my swimming trunks home with me even though I would never have a chance to wear them again. It was still dark out when I finished packing, but there was a faint smear of light on the eastern rim of land. I sat on the edge of my bed and watched the sun rise. The atmosphere on Earth makes the rays of the sun particularly pink and lovely. I would miss many things.

I wondered what Tonia would miss.

I heard Martha get up and a few minutes later I smelled the coffee brewing. I have come to like coffee. I enjoy the light buzz it gives to my body. A little push in the morning. I walked out to join her.

Martha was sitting at the dining room table, stirring her coffee and staring into it. When she heard me, she looked up. "Your last day on Earth," she said.

"Yes."

"Mission accomplished?"

"Yes, I think so."

"I'm sorry."

I didn't say anything. Our feelings are so far apart it wasn't worth trying to discuss them.

She got up and poured me a cup of coffee and handed it to me. "We kept our part of the bargain. I expect you to keep yours. Where is the news from our daughter, Ruth?"

I pulled the packet out of my pants pocket. First I handed her a photograph. It showed a smiling daughter with two children, two boys, in her lap.

"Oh, my god," Martha's voice broke. "Look at her. Just look at her. Isn't she beautiful?"

"Yes," I agreed, even though I knew she wasn't talking to me.

"And she's had two lovely children."

I would not tell her of the fifty children Ruth wasn't allowed to keep. When I left home, she was pregnant with five girls. A rare and wondrous pregnancy.

"She looks so healthy," Martha commented, stroking the photo.

"Oh, she's very healthy. She is very well taken care of."

She had only suffered two major depressions so far. We have the medications to take care of that.

"But will she ever be able to come home?"

I hated to give Martha false hope, but I told her what I knew. "There is a chance. Not for quite a while, but maybe in twenty, twenty-five years."

Martha's face crumpled. "I don't understand. Why so long? I'll probably be dead by then!"

Her daughter would not be allowed to leave until she went through menopause and was no longer able to bear children. Or until we, as a society, were able to clone children successfully and with genetic variety. My father was working on that.

"How is her husband?" Martha asked.

"He's doing very well. He is very well thought of in our society." Unfortunately, they were not really a couple any longer. Her daughter had picked another man to have her children with the second time, and the last few times she was artificially inseminated. She didn't seem to like anyone except her children anymore.

"What does she do to keep busy?" Martha asked.

"I really don't know. I met her only briefly. I think she cares for the children."

"Why did you take her to your planet?"

"We needed her. We need new blood on our planet. But we did not take her by force."

Martha bent her head. "Yes. I know. I know she was in love. But she also wanted to be a chemical engineer. Has she gone on to school?"

"I think it is available to her." I pulled a letter out of my pocket. "She has written to you."

Martha held it in her hand like it was fragile. Then she looked at me and said, "Excuse me, but I think I'd like to be alone when I read this."

I already knew what it said. Nothing that would break her mother's heart; little of Ruth's real life was revealed. I took my cup of coffee and went and sat on the front steps. The sun had risen. I would leave this world in just over twelve hours. At sunset. I told Tonia to meet me here. Then we would walk to the place we would depart from.

I thought of Tonia. Would she become like Ruth after she had had twenty children? Would she hate me? I hadn't really told her what her life would be like. She would need to get pregnant as soon as we got back home. She would then stay pregnant most of the rest of her life until she could no longer have children. She would be well fed and well taken care of, but she wouldn't be allowed much freedom. She would only be allowed to keep three children. And only boys. The girls were too valuable. She would never even see them. They would be taken from her at birth.

I had thought of all of this before theoretically, but now I thought of it with Tonia in mind. She would hate it.

I had only read about love before.

I love my father and my brothers.

I love my land.

But what I feel for Tonia is beyond all this.

I love her more than I had known was possible.

I stared at the sun. I would never see this sun again, feel this particular warmth, after I left Earth. I would miss it.

Branko told me to take little with me. I looked at the pile on my bed. I had taken one book, *A Christmas Carol.* There would be no Christmas where I was going. I was bringing several photographs of my family. A sweater that my mother knit me. A drawing of a rose that my father had done for me when I was a kid. An old teddy bear. Trying to pack made me realize how much I was leaving behind. I had to pretend this was only a trip, a vacation, going to meet Branko's family, and then someday I would be back. Otherwise, I wouldn't be able to leave.

I wore a necklace from my grandmother, my good baggy jeans, my high school sweatshirt, and my favorite pair of running shoes.

I left a letter for my parents and for Beatrice. I had taken Buzz to go get an ice cream cone earlier in the day. I let him get the biggest one and he made a complete mess with it. Then he gave me a hug. I bought flowers for my mother and made my dad his favorite muffins for dinner. I hoped they would understand someplace in their hearts. I wrote them, as Branko had instructed me, to contact the police, but not to tell them the truth. I would be just one in a million missing teenage girls.

I hadn't gone to see Beatrice today. I called her and

told her I wasn't sure yet if I was leaving with Branko. I just couldn't face her. She is my best friend. I will never know anyone like her again. Where I am going no one will know me. I will never be able to sit and have toast and read books with her, make up words with her. But of everyone in my life, I thought she would understand the most why I was doing this. I was especially glad that she had Walter in her life now.

I cleaned my room.

I took a bath.

I waited until five o'clock and then I left with my stuff in a gym bag. I waved good-bye to my parents and said I wouldn't be too late. I hoped they wouldn't worry too much. They smiled at me. I tried to take a last memory photograph of their faces. I love them so much. I will miss them forever.

I walked down the street and felt the air of Earth weighing on my shoulders. Would the atmosphere be different there? Would there be plants and flowers? I hadn't asked Branko so many things. What about other animals? I kept walking, forcing my feet forward. I was scared. But I was also excited. I was doing something that few people had done before. I was leaving Earth to live on another planet. Thinking of myself as an explorer helped—like Columbus, like Magellan, like the ancient people who walked over the Bering Strait when it was land to come to North America. It was as big a step for them.

Branko and I will be together the rest of my life. I am going on a great adventure.

When I got to the house where Branko was staying, I stopped out front and noticed how dark it looked. The sun was almost down. The light was a soft mauve color that shaded the trees and the sky was a darker purple. I took a deep breath, thinking of what I was about to do.

Then, I ran up the front walk and knocked on the door.

An older woman answered the door. "Yes?" she said.

"I am here for Branko. I'm supposed to meet him."

"He left."

I felt like someone had pulled the moon out of my belly. I felt like I was floating in space. "He left?"

"Yes."

"But I was supposed to go with him."

The woman shut her eyes for a moment and then stared at me hard. "You're lucky you're not going. You don't need to become a baby machine."

"But I love him."

"You're young. You will love a few more people before you die."

"But I wanted to go."

"He left this for you." She handed me a note.

I took the note and crumpled it in my hand and walked away. I walked to the middle of the street. I would have run after him, but I didn't know where to go. I walked over and sat on the curb and read the note:

My most beautiful Tonia. I love you too much. If I loved you a little less, you would be with me. I cannot do this to you. Believe me. I will always be with you. I think of you forever. You are in my heart and in my bones. I will miss you like the water that we swam in. I will miss you until I close my eyes the last time. Believe me. You are loved. My Tonia. Branko.

I put the letter in my gym bag. I cried. Cars drove slowly past me. I didn't care. The lady came and stared at me from the sidewalk. I waved her away. After it was completely dark and only the stars sang in the sky, I got up and walked home.

My parents were watching TV when I got home. I waved at them. They smiled. I walked upstairs. Buzz was sleeping. I opened his door and looked in on him. I was glad to see them all. It was not supposed to be this way. I wanted to tell them what I had almost done. I wanted to give them the gift of me back. But I couldn't. They didn't need to know.

I went into my room and lay facedown on my bed. I wrapped my arms around me and remembered Branko. I had to believe I would never forget him. I had the letter. I would keep it with me. I slept with it next to my face. When I slept, I dreamed of the sky turning from blue to black and opening into a huge mouth as wide as a scream. I woke up in my bed and held on to the sheets.

◉°∴ ◖BRANKO

The sky is so dark. It isn't really the sky, it is the outer space. We are deep in it in our transportation ship. We are all ready to go under for the long flight home. We are bringing back five females. There are two of us who were unsuccessful. No one looks at us or talks to us. Two of the females have become friends already and are giggling nervously like birds. One is crying. One is holding on tightly to her boyfriend. The last one is sitting very quietly, watching everything.

I know, in a very deep sense, that I have failed. I know that all my life I will never be allowed to forget my failure. The emptiness I feel for Tonia is like a cloud that surrounds me. But in part of myself I am singing. I am talking to Tonia in our language and I am telling her that I have done a good action for her. I know she will understand someday.

Branko has been gone for a month. It's early September. School starts in a week. My parents took Buzz and me to the state fair yesterday. A real family outing. I went on the Ferris wheel and closed my eyes and pretended I was flying through the stars. Then Buzz grabbed my hand and pulled me to Earth.

It's a little cold to be swimming, but I wanted to go one last time.

No one is on the beach but me.

I walk slowly into the water. I feel the coolness touch my ankles, my knees, my thighs, up over my hipbones, and then I dive in. It is a shock. This lake is the only other world I'll ever enter. I swim as long as I can underwater without breathing and then I come up for air.

I turn over on my back and float. They say if you go down into a deep well even in the daytime you can see the stars in the sky. I sink into the water, keeping my eyes open. I let out air until I'm under and I keep staring up at the sky.

He's beyond the water. He's beyond the blue. He's through the dark and the stars. He's home.

I saved him.

Then he saved me.

It's enough.

I come up for air.